A Beacon of Hope

Jaspher Rori

"It is Great to be Great, but is Greater to be Human"
- Will Rogers, 1879~1935

First Edition: November 2011
Published by Nsemia Inc. Publishers (www.nsemia.com)

Edited By: Sheena Brennan
Cover Concept & Illustration: Jaspher Rori
Cover Design: Danielle Pitt
Layout Design: Kemunto Matunda

Note for Librarians:
A cataloguing record for this book is available from Library and Archives Canada.

ISBN: 978-1-926906-14-0

DEDICATION

For you my beloved children: Moraa, Lenah, Linda and Jimmy. You have a special place in my heart, and I have big dreams and a lot of hopes for you in the days ahead. Hard work, patience and morality have no substitute in life. Great men and women have had to endure hardship to succeed. As you navigate through life, so, do it wisely and in the end you will be rewarded abundantly.

Acknowledgements

To God, glory and honour is yours. I wish to express my immense appreciation and gratitude to all those who helped me to write this book. The ideas herein were gathered and rejuvenated in my interactions with peers. In particular, I sincerely acknowledge the role played by Journalist Jimmy Achira, author of *Mwakenya: Real or Phantom? A Journalist's Harrowing Experiences in the Moi Regime*, for having encouraged me to complete this work and his efforts to introduce me to the publisher who overreadily received my work. I appreciate the role played by my friends, Andrew Moreka, Charles Orenge (Sibour), Isaiah Nyakundi, and Jeffy Ogeto, the Kisii based computer software administrators who were handy when my laptop "misbehaved" and helped in editing, formatting and designing the book; and Carol Wallace (Imenti) who initially typed the manuscript. I cannot forget Mary Arap Chuma, the parents of Jimmy Highway Academy, in Nyamira County, for their songs and encouragement. Last but not least, I pay my glowing tribute to Dr Matunda Nyanchama, the publisher of **Nsemia. Inc. publishers**, for his encouragement, reading my manuscript and agreeing to publish it.

About the Author

Jaspher Rori was born in West Mugirango, Nyamira County, Kenya. He studied at Moi Forces Academy and University of Nairobi, graduating with a degree in Agriculture. He later obtained a diploma in Project Management from Kenya Institute of Management. Presently he is enrolled in post-graduate studies in Project Planning and Management at the University of Nairobi.

Jaspher has worked as a high school teacher, and a manager in the tea industry in Kenya. He likes writing on a number of themes with special interest in Gusii history, culture, proverbs and sayings. He credits this passion to his parents and grandparents who were keen storytellers with many of these tales shared in evening fireside chats.

Jaspher is currently working on *The Eye of Mayenga*, a novel set in a typical African village and captures challenges of life in such an environment. This is in addition to his interest in *Gusii History, Culture, Proverbs and Sayings*.

Foreword

At the advent of colonialism, many African communities resisted the external incursion into their territories, and the associated intrusion to their culture by the colonialists. Instead, many opted to stick to their own ways of life. However, there were individuals who abandoned their culture, religion and collaborated with the colonists. In turn, they received privileges such as taking their children to school. Invariably, the educated ended up reaping the gains of education. At the dawn of Kenya's independence in 1963, they were the most qualified to occupy positions of leadership and take the available jobs.

When Jomo Kenyatta became the prime minister of Kenya, the glaring issues he promised to tackle were poverty, diseases and ignorance. Thus, modern education was perceived as the escape route from these vices; and there was rush for it.

Unfortunately, other ills of society emerged later such as negative ethnicity, nepotism, corruption, patronage, and politics with largely negative impacts, among others. These vices largely resulted in a situation where available resources and jobs became a preserve of the "elite class" in society, pretty much locking out those with neither means nor access to the elite class; and this, despite one's qualifications.

With the rampant practices of these vices, private and public institutions became a preserve of the privileged class who looted and mismanaged them with archetypical abandon. Coupled with the global economic recession and stringent measures from the international community, the economy slackened further shutting the doors to many available for jobs. The dreams of many jobseekers were thrown into oblivion. Then, education "ceased" being the luster it was. The modern graduate who was trained for a white collar job found himself or herself struggling to beat the odds to survive.

Jaspher brings out these challenges candidly leaving society to question itself: Where have we come from? Where are we now? Where shall we be in future?

Ruth Sarange Nyachoti, Bsc. Nursing, Msc. Public Health
Nairobi, Kenya

Chapter One

The whole village of Manga to the south of Lake Victoria and to the east of Kisii town was for once engulfed in one of the most unique celebrations there had ever been. For the first time in their history since the advent of the modern education; the education brought in by the white men to "teach and give hope to the people" as they put it, the village was getting their first university graduate. That was close to a hundred years since the first white men came to Gusiiland.

It was not that there were no schools in Manga, nor that the village failed to send their children to school. No.

Around 1905 when the first British colonialists arrived in Gusiiland, they found the local population deeply engrossed in their cultural activities and way of life. It was a simple life with challenges, yet satisfying. They were farming, holding ceremonies, praying and giving sacrifices to their god and ancestors who directed their lives. There were established systems for learning about all they needed to learn. In times of war, the young men came out to repulse the enemy and protect the people and wealth.

Shortly after, in 1911, the white Catholic missionaries followed and established a Catholic church at Nyabururu, about three kilometres away from Kisii town. Local people fondly called it Nyabororo. Many converted to the new faith. They built a primary school there to serve the surrounding villages. In 1913, another group of missionaries from Kamagambo and Bugema, in Uganda, arrived with the same message of salvation and built a Seventh Day Adventist (SDA) church and a primary school at Nyanchwa, on one of the hills surrounding Bosongo (Kisii town). Apart from preaching about the salvation and the second coming of Jesus Christ, they asked the people to abandon their god who was non-existent, they said, converting souls to Christ and asking them to abandon their culture terming it "meaningless retrogressive lifestyles and practices."

The two mainstream churches encouraged the people to embrace the white man's education, way of life and God. With the white man's education, they said, one stood a chance to transform his or her life for the better. With a new way of life, one kept diseases and old age at bay, and lived a better and longer life, so they said. And with Christ, one was assured of everlasting life. They were told all they were doing was rubbish. They sang: "All good, all good in education. Come and see, come and see. Come and sing, come and sing. Tempt it, tempt it." All these were meant to entice the community to accept the new education and take it seriously.

However, the messages did not go down well with everybody. More new schools and churches sprout up all over the land. More white people came in to preach the new faith and teach the new education. Those who had accepted the new teaching and gone to school became teachers after learning the basics of reading and writing. Their lives, mannerism and style seemed to change for the better, but they were seen with parted breath.

There was curiosity in the village. "Come one come all, and you will have eternal life." The message from the Catholic fathers and the men of God echoed across the ranges and swept across Gusiiland like bush fire. "There is hope for better life," they argued. Diseases were treated using modern medicine and the new faith assured people of a land, Canaan; a land of honey, milk flowing unabated, sweet fruits, singing and dancing around the throne, and where people will never die when Jesus, the son of God, comes back a second time to take His chosen ones.

Indeed, the message was enticing. But the Gusii had

known *engoro*, their god, as the source of life, all knowing, all present and all powerful. He and only he directed their lives and knew even where the wind slept. He lived high beyond the sky from where he watched over them and directed their lives. He was a god of mercy and plenty, and when not pleased with the people, he rained disaster as a lesson. Therefore, they knew how to please him through regular sacrifices and rituals.

They were told that the God of the white man was more powerful than *engoro*. And *engoro* did not exist but was an idol of worship. If he existed he would burn in hell with the sinners who refused to worship Christ, and those who drank beer, sniffed tobacco, smoked and broke the Ten Commandments. Those who accepted Jesus as their saviour were assured of everlasting life; a life without misery, hardship or hard work, but filled with flowing honey and milk, and time spent rejoicing and singing around the throne. Those who did not accept Christ were to burn in a hail of fire for a thousand years when Jesus Christ returned a second time to take his chosen ones. Those who embraced Him would live forever without fear: fear of constant raids from the Kipsigis and Maasai, for their cattle, pastureland, women and children; hailstones, mysterious diseases, hunger and even death. He was a loving and merciful God of plenty and a God above all gods. He was more powerful than *engoro* and the ancestors.

Sakagwa, the prophet of the Abagusii who lived between 1830 and 1902, had foretold of the coming of the white men. He warned the Gusii not to fight them. "People who look like butterflies will come from the lake. Do not offer resistance. They will kill you if you fight them as they will have superior weapons that spit fire. But they will stay amongst us and finally leave us to rule ourselves," Sakagwa told his people on multiple occasions. "Button mushrooms will sprout at Getembe and only those with men will harvest them." He advised his people to take their children to school to learn the secrets of the white men: education, so that they could equip themselves to harvest the button mushrooms. However, by the time the white men arrived, they had forgotten Sakagwa's prophesy.

People responded to the calls with mixed feelings. Some saw the new comers with suspicion, urging them to discard their religion, the god of their ancestors and follow a God of the foreigners who they did not understand. They were being urged to abandon their culture and traditions and follow the alien ones. With these, they were simply going against *engoro* and their ancestors. They were inviting curses amongst themselves and would have no way to cleanse them. Even sacrifices wouldn't do. They argued. *Engoro* and the ancestors would be too displeased with them to have any mercy, let alone to accept their sacrifices and rituals.

Taking local brew and circumcision of their girls were sins according to the white men. Yet these practices were age old customs, practised by their forefathers, and *engoro* had had mercy on them over the years. He had seen them from mystic Misri, the cradle of mankind through Congo, Agwassi and Kano plains; Kabianga as their ancestors sojourned to their present land, Gusii highland. Many questions lingered unanswered. How will a girl become a woman without being circumcised? How will the people have a past time and hold ceremonies without local brew? How will the ancestors and *engoro* be made happy without regular praises and sacrifices? How sure were they that the new God, the God of the white men could be trusted to protect them against life's adversities? Aren't they the same people brutalizing us over what was considered our heritage? Have they not taken our land and openly coveted our women? Those who got sick visited Gwako, the renowned medicine-man to cure their illnesses and afflictions. As usual, some were cured and continued with their normal lives while some died, just like those treated in the white men's hospitals.

No, not many people were enticed with the good promises

and messages of salvation to abandon their culture and traditions. There were suspicions and lack of goodwill in their eyes. Not even the fear of death and sinners burning in hell for a thousand years scared or enticed them. One man who was not happy with what was happening was Otenyo. Otenyo lived with his aunt in the outskirts of Bosongo. He was unhappy with the way the white men took their fertile land, brutalized them, took their cattle, contradicted their culture and ruled them with an iron fist. He openly resisted this white man's rule. He and his group sang, "*aeta amare, omwana bw'omosongo aete amare, ee; ndege manwari*", meaning, "let him pass in the sky, the child of a white man, can he pass over the sky with his powerful plane." In defiance, Otenyo drank *busaa*, a local brew, took his spear and killed District Governor Northcorthe who was riding on a horse. Moraa Ng'iti and Nyamacharara who were the progenitors of Sakagwa led a rebellion against the colonists. They recruited young men to form *Enyamumbo*, an underground movement to fight and chase the white men and regain their land and sovereignty.

Some took the new messages positively, perhaps out of fear, desire for change and new experiences. They accepted the new God, abandoned and discarded *engoro* the god of Abagusii, and were immediately recruited to baptism classes. They wanted to have eternal life; life in the new home, Canaan. They stopped brewing and drinking beer and giving prayers to their god and ancestors. They embraced education, and sent their children to school. Of course these were sacrifices. There were prices to pay. Their cows had to go hungry, and gardens had to be abandoned as their children who were their source of labour went to school. There were fees to pay and ridicule to bear from those diehards who felt that these people had betrayed their god, culture and the traditions of their ancestors to embrace an alien religion and culture. It was a matter of time before the ancestors and *engoro* rained their wrath with indomitable vengeance. They reasoned. Those who embraced the new religion stopped giving regular sacrifices to *engoro*. They reduced their associations with non-believers. Instead, they met regularly to sing hymns in praise of the white man's God, as they called Him, and give ten percent of their harvest to church, to encourage one another and listen to the good news. They abandoned their culture and traditions. When they felt sick, they went to white men's hospitals to be treated and sought God's intervention for their afflictions. They stopped visiting medicine-men and could not take herbs as they were considered a sin. Their water for drinking was boiled to kill germs and some stopped eating meat for reasons that were not clear.

Others were lukewarm to the good news. They were baptized, regularly attended church services to satisfy curiosity, and they sent their children to school, but quietly held to their customs and traditions. Boys looked after cattle and their attendances in school were irregular while girls continued with their routines as a source of labour, and when they were of age, were quietly circumcised and married off to provide wealth to their families. They prayed to *engoro* and the ancestors, giving regular sacrifices to them and held rituals as customs dictated, as they did not want to offend their god and their ancestors. They were not too sure with the new God and His messages. They secretly consulted medicine-men and diviners to solve their problems and attended hospitals at will, and often as a last resort when sick. They brewed and drank beer in secrecy and sang traditional songs at night just like the non-converts.

Manga remained lukewarm. Some elders and children attended church services religiously in the morning for curiosity sake and in the evening enjoyed their local brew singing praises to *engoro* and the ancestors. Children carried on with their chores and played age old games: hide and seek, *onyuro,* sliding on wet tree grooves, building makeshift-huts out of twigs and branches, putting bird snares and hunting for rabbits and antelopes in the ranges. Some children attended school as a matter of fact, routinely: To satisfy curiosity with no parental guidance. "Go to school and play with others." A mother would ignorantly tell her child as she saw it off to school. This continued on even after independence from the British rule in 1963. Those who went very far in school only dropped out in the early classes of secondary school; the highest level someone from the village had ever realized. Some parents were even happy that the burden of school fees was off-loaded when children dropped out of school. With poverty ravaging the village, the cost of secondary education was an uphill task to many parents. And with these, the village found itself caught up in a disadvantaged position compared with neighbouring villages, which at an early stage had conformed to the changing trends, embraced education and were now reaping the fruits Sakagwa the prophet had foretold. They had accepted to take their children to school, sacrificed to pay school fees and year in and year out churned graduates from various universities and colleges. These graduates took up jobs in the public service and later sought positions of leadership in the society. The message of education as a serious undertaking sunk in slowly and much later in Manga.

Thus, the celebration centered on hope and perceived liberation from the past: the many anguishes and unaccomplished promises the village had not enjoyed, all in the pretext that they had not taken education seriously. They had not heeded the advice to discard their so-called retrogressive approach to life and embraced modern trends to earn the fruits that came with it: so it was said. The celebration supposedly marked a breakthrough to the world of education that was to usher in new perceptions and new thinking; new challenges, new opportunities and a torrential flow of the attendant juices and honey to all the people of Manga village.

It was always the other villages that produced a member of parliament, or a councilor come the general election, irrespective of their distaste and voting as a block. Even the local sub-chief and chief came from the other villages. Thus, they were spectators in all matters appertaining to their welfare. Why? They had none in the village who had the right education to qualify for these positions. None from the village had contested for a seat or with qualifications to seek any office.

Progress was an ambiguous word to the village. It was an aspect only enjoyed by other villages. Yet, they were their neighbours sharing a tie, a cord, an ancestor, a stream or a market, a school, an administrative unit and many others. Honour and respect from the other villagers never existed in reality. The village itself had the most dishonourable nick names. They were termed laggards, thick-headed, good-for-nothing idiots who failed to live in reality of the changing times. Many other labels were said behind their backs. Whether earned or not, for God's sake, they knew, they weren't pleasant nick names. They knew they had trailed behind. Even in the chief's meetings, not even an elder sat nearer the chief or constituted his council of elders. They felt condemned to playing subservient roles to the other villages. In such meetings, their roles were to lend their ears, and take instructions from above that trickled in rather alien formats. They clapped and applauded these sophisticated and exclusive approaches with disquiet in their hearts and a longing that their own son or daughter should too be seated in one of those seats. But they knew too well that that was only possible if they had children who had qualifications just like them.

Nobody from the village ever owned a car, had a prestigious job in the civil service or the private sector, or a had political slot to add a feather to the village. Nobody spoke highly of them. And when the fruits of their labour trickled down, through government or non-governmental organizations, it was said, usually in hushed voices, that most had ended up in undeserving pockets. Whether these were mere hearsay or not, the talk was rife in the lips of all. Not a single road was passable through the Manga village, yet the other villages had electricity.

So when Musa coiled his way to university, the village of Manga was rife with hope. It was a delight, a sigh of relief and a hope for better things to come not only to his family, but to the entire village of Manga. He was their beacon of hope. They felt that with time, their own son would propel them to higher heights: To make them respected amongst their neighbours, and usher in a new beginning; a beginning of hope and dreams unrealized. If one said the village had no one who had gone to school, they would say, "no, see, we too have a son with a degree." He was an impetus to the parents and the young generation to play their respective roles of taking education seriously.

Chapter Two

Mogaka, Musa's father sat on a pile of dried wood just outside his grass-thatched house. Slowly and thoughtfully sipped his traditional beer from one big calabash made of finger millet straws, *ekemunu*. He watched as the village young men put in the last preparations to mark the crowning of Musa, his first born son, as the hope of the village. He was already feeling tired from the many days and nights of sleeplessness spent in preparations for this great occasion. Several elders sat next to him on their three-legged stools forming a semi-circle and drinking beer from one big pot, *embiru*, using long slender bamboo straws. They probed from one topic to another giving credit or openly discrediting a point. They thanked God for the favourable weather but not the frequent hailstones that wreaked havoc on ripe crops in the fields. Nyakundi, his elder brother sat beside him with his long unkempt grey beard, an old black suit with an old long oversized black coat, *rimana ng'ombe*, covering his knees. His head was partially covered with white hair: evidence that he had seen seasons behind him.

The morning sun was already high and as usual its heat burning. Mogaka looked towards the river: down his piece of land. His *shamba* ran from the top of the hill like a strip of road to the lower part of Manga stream. Here, a small swamp constantly supplied water reeds, *esasati,* for thatching houses. Though its width was small, its mere length was appreciable. He could not have complained much about land had he not married two wives. These were *Mobucha ibu*, the first wife and mother to Musa, and *Nyamesancho*, his second wife. Both had blessed him with several children, meaning many mouths to feed, yet giving him immense status as an elder. He was wealthy and regarded highly amongst villagers. Many children were a symbol of wealth and status. He was one of the villagers with relatively a bigger share of land now that land had become scarce with the increase of people. When he was a child, every man held a big chunk of land. Most of it was uncultivated. Cattle, sheep and goats roamed freely across the range. In the evening, every animal found its way home unguided. A remnant of wild animals in the nearby bushes provided a constant supplement of nutrients. But now, he wondered that the generations to come might have nothing to inherit.

The upper part of his land was bare, with boulder-type rocks sunken in infertile soils. It was covered with very scanty grass, short shrubs and countable short trees that had a strong will to live. It was a known obstinate piece and in his hey days a wife who could not toe his line was allocated such a section to till. The idea was to soften her tough and bloated head. It produced little food, if any. However, it had been a useful playing ground for young children. He recalled himself playing there: hide and seek, sliding on wet pieces of wood and constructing temporary make-shift-twig huts with his friends. He played with them until dark. As it was the norm, fun always ended at sunset when the little boys and girls dismantled their twig-made huts to signal the end of the day. The games never ended without a tear. Some naughty boys, who could not accept defeat, pinched others, called them names or ran away with their items leaving them crying and shouting names in return. It was in such scenario that one came to learn that he had a big head or a bad nickname. And somehow, that was great fun. In the month of March, *egetamo nyamorero mobariri*, there was intense heat. Fierce mysterious fires emerged from nowhere. They burned the scanty vegetation and left the ground bare. It was said that *chisokoro*, the ancestors themselves lit the fire to warm themselves. Brown dust emerged from the ground to the sky, blown by strong winds from the lake. This signalled that the planting season was over. Then in April, *rigwata*, there was torrential rain that filled the streams and rivers, germinating the millet sown in the fields.

Midway down, he had built his homestead securely surrounded by the injurious cacti fence and leaving only one entrance to it. This accorded him extra security from frequent cattle raiders from Moromba. Together with his "cobras of Mwabogonko," as he called his tall, dark sons, Mogaka enhanced his security from the constant cattle raids from the Kalenjin warriors, and Maasai morans (*Abamanyi*) and other clans of Gusii. The cattle boma was built at the centre of his homestead. He woke up three times a night to ensure the cows were safe from the numerous cattle rustlers who never respected the idea that even a new born child needed milk.

Mogaka grew a variety of crops normally for subsistence. In times of good yields, he sold some to augment his income. Sometimes he was better off than his neighbours. Unfortunately, he had many needs to meet. He had many mouths to feed, schools fees to pay, clothes to buy, rituals to appease *engoro*, and the ancestors, ceremonies to hold and many uncountable things to do with this meager produce and income.

A small footpath led further down his land to where his zebu cows amply munched green pasture. His flock had diminished with time. There was not enough land to keep many cows and goats. Unlike before, when they were dying from tick related diseases, now the challenge was on lack of pasture land. A tributary of river Manga ran at the bottom, naturally separating Manga from Girango. Young boys from Girango and Manga always met at the river to bathe and swim in its shallow waters. Here they played with its waters fought over ridge supremacy and in rage called each other unprintable names. This was toned down to whose father was a great wrestler, had many cows and children, or was a wizard. The boys of Manga became aware at a young age that their parents were no comparison to the parents of the other villages. The parents of Manga were damn drunkards, lazy, ravaged with poverty and did not value education. But the two neighbours remained friends. Their relationship was further cemented by several intermarriages. Cows were always going to that ridge and coming back. As the elders put it, *chiombe makabe, chiare kogenda chiairana, chisangia Mwasi na onde mware motamanyaini*, cows go round and come back, and make people from afar meet others they could have never met and known.

With these intermarriages, the two neighbours somehow had a reason to respect one another. The elders greeted one another in a special way. They were in-laws, sisters, brothers, grandmothers or grandfathers. When they met, one could watch in admiration how they shook hands in prolonged embrace. They called one another respectable names and inquired how their families were fairing across the ridges.

Mogaka admired his elder brother Nyakundi, a respected medicine-man, sitting next to him. He was an epitome of wisdom. Although age had caught up with him, he was still quite energetic and intelligent. Perhaps, he reasoned it was because he did not have a lot on his hands. All his children were grown up and none were in school. Even with that, he did not see much good in education. All his sweat went down his stomach. He was considered to have travelled widely. In his youth, he fought alongside the white men in Burma. When he returned home, he had learnt to speak some broken English, and Kiswahili. When their father was suddenly called to join the world of ancestors one morning, as the eldest son, he took his mantle. He steered the family as if the old man was still around and watching. He united them when differences emerged to tear them apart. He raised their spirits when moments were tough. Over the years Nyakundi remained respectable, always giving wise counsel to the village. In the mornings, a stream of people flocked his home for a cure, and divination, a trade he inherited from their father. He dispensed herbal concoctions, *emete anchogu*, divined their fortunes and gave them hope to live. In return, his services were paid with goats and sometimes cows. He was relatively well-to-do, but such animals are better off for domestic use, paying bride price and not to enrich oneself or paying school fees. So, he used them to marry six wives who gave him several children.

Nyakundi drew Mogaka's attention. He spoke with a melancholic tone, with his lips playing and his face wearing an unequivocal smile. He cleared his throat. "The journey was long."

"Indeed Nairobi is far, elder," Mogaka agreed with him. "I never thought I would ever reach there. Musa has made possible for all of us to cross the ridges and see the big city we only heard stories about and heard over the radio." The other elders nodded their heads in agreement.

"The big city with many roads, tall houses, floods of light and people swarming like butterflies. Life is not ordinary there. It's a total contrast to the village life," Monda, another elder added his voice.

"No wonder why our children who go there stay long and forget to come back to see us," Atandi remarked as he drew his beer. "They get corrupted with the life of the city; women wearing tight trousers and walking almost naked. Can these women allow our sons to come home to marry?"

"They say that is the way of civilization. For us anything above the knee is private," Mogaka noted.

"Then, flies and heaps of garbage emitting an awful stench that can easily drive away flies themselves and choke one's throat. Ooh the stench could easily suffocate. You saw how I sneezed the whole day," Nyakundi held his nose high, and said in disgust as he sniffed his tobacco.

"Remember I coughed all the way back, yet tobacco sniffers do not cough or sneeze twice. For a moment, I felt lonely. I missed the nostalgic scent of the countryside, the humming trees, the cracking flow of river Manga and its frogs, the endless dirges of birds and the freedom of children playing and running errands."

"And the semi-naked children; competing with crows, scavenging from heaps of garbage. Don't they have homes and parents? Is the government just watching lives rot away?" Mogaka wondered as he sipped his beer again.

"Crows and vultures are a bad omen, remember," Nyakundi interjected. "They are a product of the loose life of the city. These are bad signs of things to come. Crows and vultures are not clean birds," Nyakundi shook his head slowly. Then, as if possessed by some spirit, he said, "show me a girl in the village with a child out of wedlock," he continued. "Show me one, who has failed to be married or marry, and I will compose a song in her or his honour?" he posed. "I'll sing myself hoarse if I saw one. When Marita, daughter of Kiage, went to town and came back with a baby boy, we asked her who the father was. Marita said nothing. We retreated to our huts with other elders and by evening we had a song, "*rikong'o ndire ng'umbu eria. Rinyenyere embori ring'anye,* there is an old cow across. Slaughter a goat for it to leave". This was a mockery to make her start evaluating herself. The same evening when we had taken our beer, we sang ourselves hoarse. I soloed. The next morning, the song was in the lips of even a child born yesterday. The boys sang it as they drove cows home and girls as they fetched water or firewood."

"And she moved to her home," Kiage interjected as he nodded his head.

Elder Nyakundi continued, "as if that was the medicine, the trick worked. The next weeks were a heap of activities in elder Kiage's house. Word had gotten around and two groups came to Kiage's home seeking Marita's hand in marriage."

Kiage picked from there, "one was an old man, Nyamiaka Omonyamwaka, who had been away from home for a long time and refused to marry. When he heard that there was a beautiful girl for marriage, he summoned a few of his friends, carried their walking sticks, and trailed their legs like ferns to my home. We asked him for only six cows, and one bull, *eeri y'egesicho gose y'obokombe* and one goat, *embori y'egetumbe.* Nyamiaka, a much disorganized man had only two cows. Who could give out his daughter for only two cows? Even if I was aware that my daughter could not marry a man of her age and status as her leg had been broken. 'Let it be,' I said loudly. Two days later, *enda nyakebari,* you know him for his big stomach, came to me and offered to pay twelve cows, a bull and a goat, double what I had asked Nyamiaka. I accepted and Marita moved out of our home to be the fourth wife to Chief Nyamweya. She is now old in her home, respectable, and with her eight children and grandchildren."

The elders were in agreement. A badly behaved girl waited for a man from afar who did not know her character, and one who had a child out of wedlock married an old man or one with other wives. She never could have the privilege of being the respected first wife. This created social control and order. That is the only hope for society. "That is why our culture has always had something good," elder Nyakundi added.

A young man came with quick steps from an open field to where the elders were seated. He respectfully informed them, "elders, the stage is set for the ceremony. The chairs have been arranged and the high table placed. The villagers have assembled and taken their seats."

As usual in Manga, during any ceremony there was a lot of food to eat. Cows and goats were slaughtered. Women brewed beer in pots for the elders. The climax of it all were the speeches where ideas were shared. These were followed with belts of songs and dances. The elders advised the youngsters on how to carry on with life. And the youngsters were expected to heed these pieces of advice. Well, the elders had lived longer giving them a couple of experiences to borrow from: some good and others bad.

The elders stood up from their chairs one after the other and slowly walked with the support of their walking sticks in a single file to the venue in an open field a few metres in front of Mogaka's homestead. There was a big gathering with women and children singing and dancing. They joined them in several jigs, twisting their shoulders and legs. Musa was the focus. He was praised in many songs for ushering in the new light to the village of Manga. He danced with them. He was dressed in traditional attire: a colourful cap made of a monkey skin, a black pair of trousers, a white shirt and a coat made from leopard skin. He moved his head up and down with the rhythm of the songs. He wore a convincingly confident smile. He had conquered where none in the village had tried to conquer.

At the centre was a three-legged stool decorated with assorted colours of beads and shiny cowry shells. Beside was a thick shield made of buffalo skin, a spear, a sword placed in a pouch, a small brownish milk gourd and a small pot with traditional liquor. Elders took their seats in front of the crowd. Musa sat next to his father, Mogaka, who wore an air of importance. He had sacrificed to see his son through school. The rest of the villagers sat down on the grass. The small pot with traditional brew and a gourd with fermented milk were placed next to Nyakundi. All the eyes were fixed on Musa.

Nyakundi stamped his authority by flying his fly whisky several times in the air. "Manga *oiyee*. Manga *oiyeee*. Manga *oiyeeee*," he shouted at the top of his voices. In unison, the crowd roared back in thundering voices, "*oiyeeee*." Then the crowd was drowned in deafening quietness. He cleared his throat and with the charismatic gaiety, shouted, "Manga *oiyee*. Manga *oiyee*." The crowd roared back again in unison, "*oiyeeee*."

He proceeded to brief the villagers on their long journey to Nairobi, the big city, to attend Musa's graduation ceremony. He praised Musa for his hard work and perseverance that had seen him achieve the highest level of education none in the village had achieved. He had a degree none in the village had acquired. It was initially a preserve of the neighbouring villages. Not that they were better breeds than them. No. They had all come from the same ancestor, Mogusii. From the early moments they had seen the value of education and had taken it seriously, and the results were evident for all to see. They had teachers, pastors, doctors and in every election time they produced a member of parliament, and councillors. And every time they asked for their share, the answer was one. Manga had no one with a good enough education to fit in any position. Now they had one in Musa. Musa was likened to Monto, who long ago, led the Gusii people from the dry mystical Misri, Egypt, downwards to a land of rash pasture in Congo, on their way to their present land. Musa's role therefore was to lead them from the front and shed light to the village. He was to show the village the way out of perpetual poverty, unemployment and ridicule from the surrounding villages who had embraced education earlier.

"Your brothers and sisters are unemployed. We have nothing to show except our nakedness," elder Nyakundi emphasized, "and nothing to be proud of in front of the other villages except you. You know that." He continued, "your success, my son, has now enabled me to sit and take beer across the ridge without fear of ridicule. Through your perseverance and success we have all conquered our fears and seen a new light at the end of the tunnel." Elder Nyakundi proceeded, "we crown you to be our eyes and ears." Then, he took the sword, spear and the shield and handed them to Musa: a sword and spear to his right hand the shield to his left hand. "These are symbolic," he said, "to go out there and fight the battle. The spear will conquer the enemy, and the shield will protect you."

"Sit on that stool." The elder ordered. Musa sat on the brownish beaded three-legged stool as the crowd watched and cheered. He removed the cap Musa was wearing and raised it up with his right hand for the crowd to see. "This is the cap our predecessors, our ancestors wore." He turned to Musa, spat onto the cap thrice and then placed it back on his head saying, "wear it always." He took a gourd full of beer, sipped it and sprayed on Musa's head thrice. "Commune with our ancestors always," he uttered. He took another gourd with fermented milk and blood, sipped it and sprayed it on Musa's head. "These are the keys to your success: *chiombe n'abana*, wealth and children," Nyakundi blessed him. "May you translate these successes to the whole village of Manga. Always remember your roots," he commanded, "and now take the mantle." Elder Nyakundi gave Musa a beautifully adorned fly whisk. He remarked jokingly, "this will assist you to chase the flies and sweep your way clean. May you drink safe waters wherever you may go," he concluded.

Musa remained calm throughout this occasion. He listened to the elders' advice directed at him. "A man is not complete without his own house. You are now a man. We ask you to take a girl and start your home." They advised him. "But then, not every girl who comes your way. No. We need a girl who would fit our simple life. Who can run to the river and fetch water for your mothers," they emphasized, "respect them even in their frail energy. One who ungrudgingly can run uphill and fetch for your mother firewood to light and warm her house."

Musa expected this. Already his mother had shown signs of impatience. All his age mates had their own houses with children.

"You may take a girl who has gone to school like you so that you can complement each other, but she must respect our roots," Elder Nyakundi continued.

"And who understand our ways of life," shouted another

elder. "Not the ones, who wear miniskirts, bleach their bodies like ghosts. We all refuse that."

"See my son," elder Kiage echoed in contemplative mood. "Didn't the son of Otwori across the ridge refuse to heed the advice of the elders? Where is he now? He has not even a hut in the village where he can be buried. We hear he has mansions in Nairobi. Big houses. Of what value do houses have over his roots? Does he require impregnable mansions in Nairobi, yet has no roots to be proud of?"

The crowd roared back, "no."

"We hear his mother cries every day wondering why she bore a son who forgot her and his roots. She wonders why painstaking paid his school fees," elder Kiage added.

Kerandi was in the last lap to a centurion. As a little child, he had seen the first white men arrive in the village with a Bible on one hand and a gun on the other. He stole the moment to share his pieces of wisdom. He adjusted his coat and fumbled for the most appropriate words to suit the moment. His head was grey and wisdom is said to be enshrined in the grey hairs and bald heads, but is measured too by the weight of the words put across. He chose his words carefully and prophetically. "We have sharpened for you the tools you need to face the battle with," he said. "You have a shield, a sword and a spear. In our times, these tools were to protect us from our enemies. Now a shield is a book, a spear is a pen and a sword is your intelligence to help you navigate through life. We have given you the keys to open the doors of success. Go out and use them to your advantage and to that of your people." He looked at Musa's face. "When a man goes out to hunt, those he leaves behind wait for him to come with meat. And when he finally tracks down an antelope and makes a kill, he brings home the meat to share with his people. That is how we have lived over the ages," Kerandi emphasized rhetorically, "and that is the way we expect you to live." Then he turned and pointed to the youths, who were seated a while away

21

from the elders. "Our years are spent, and our energies are sapped. You are the people of tomorrow. When we are called by our ancestors to join them, you shall take the mantle without fear. From there we shall be watching you as you carry on. Prepare yourself for the future battles by embracing education. Education is the breast milk we had all along denied our children and a breath that will give life to Manga village."

When the ceremony was over and the people had left, Musa was left to ponder over the event. He was elated by the many songs belted in his honour and praises he had received that day. However, he felt torn between a transition of the past that the elders were imposing on him and the emergent blend of culture he had been exposed to by the virtue of having attained a modern education. The two were in total conflict. He knew what was expected of him by the entire village. He had keenly taken every bit of advice. The messages were not simple and easily achievable. It called for diligence. The expectations were many and tall to surmount in the emerging trend of reality. A reality locked away from his people, and a new world order and an emergent culture of bottle-neck competition of survival of the fittest. A reality that the village was miles behind world trends, that a university degree was not all that was required to deliver the expectations of the village. However, he noted he was paying one cost of education in a village that perceived university education with awe, and as an escape route from their miseries: Where none had received it and as a consequence, had been locked out of the mainstream development.

Marrying was a good idea, he agreed. Already he had started experiencing an urge for companionship. But it was not his first priority. He needed a job and understood how difficult it had become to get one; something the elders did not know. Further, who to marry was a matter of the heart. Their expectations were based on a culture that had held back the community from embracing change, and that was soon fading away with interaction and exposure across cultural borders. He let everything rest at that and hoped that time, yes time, the greatest decision maker, would dictate his destiny.

That evening, Musa had his own time in his grass-thatched hut to further digest what had been said to him by the elders. He lay on his bed staring at the roof. The hut was evidently old, having been built for him when he was getting initiated to manhood. That was almost ten years ago. He noted he needed to construct another one. This time a descent one befitting the expected role he had been bestowed. Moonlight rays flittered in weakly from spatial gaps on the roof. He had great challenges ahead to shed in the new light as the village expected. He could only please or disappoint them. Great kings in history, he noted, had led their subjects to victory while others had led them to destruction. What Manga needed was a list he could not quite enumerate. It was not a one man job. It was a team effort over time. He did not have means nor did he know the routes to make the dreams a reality. Yet, he felt grateful for their support, and inside, a glowing spirit of determination to fulfill the expectations burned on.

College life had been life and an experience. He recalled the young and charming girl who had captured his heart. She was Judith Nyanchera Makosa. He greatly missed her. He recalled the chancellor's graduation remarks. "The government is committed to provide education to all young people; however, the economy cannot let her absorb all the graduates in the job market. As such, those who cannot get jobs in the public and private sector are advised to consider informal employment sub-sector, *jua kali,* as an alternative source of employment." This was already a reality. Unemployment rates in the country, even for university graduates, had already become a serious concern. Musa counted some of his friends who had graduated earlier. They were still in the job market; a place where one could find the unspoken evils of corruption, patronage, tribalism and nepotism. And if one wanted to quicken his steps, one needed a 'tall' person or a 'go between' to hold his or her hand. He did not have any of these. He was all alone to swim in the sea of sharks. One who has his people is held by the hand to come home. One who does not have his people is left to hold onto a dry tree, *obwate omwabo, obwatwa koboko ocha ka. Otabwati omwabo, obwata moraa mwomo.* Going by this, he knew it would take some time before lady luck knocked on his door.

With this emerging reality, and having gone to the prestigious university of Nairobi when everybody in the village of Manga saw education as the gateway to prestige and affluence, Musa felt hollow inside. He felt hopelessly cheated. Again, he thought of the elders' speeches: "you're our Moses," they had said, "look for a girl who understands our ways of life." He felt confused.

"To some extent, they are right and to some they are not." He comforted himself. He wanted someone to share with his life, someone to love and to return his love unconditionally, someone to spend the happy and sad moments together, and children too to grace the marriage. But not just a woman who would come into his life, bear children and not add value. Not one to be the source of his misery for the rest of his life.

Musa reflected to the days when his father Mogaka was strong and energetic. He called himself *aberia ambeche*, a sow or a female pig. Now he wished someone could take him back to his youth to regain his energy to gather like a sow. Mogaka always said, *"tankoria ing'irane boke borere bwa nyancha kobong'ia buna aberia ambeche,* I wish one can take me back to my youth to run and gather like a sow." Unlike other villagers, he had embraced education. He encouraged his children to go to school and provided though with strains. He was not a lazy man. He always woke up before sunrise to carry out his chores. In the evening he always brought home something for his children, be it a piece of meat, sugar or salt. But now, his energy had been sapped by age. He was overweight with school fees for a number of his children in primary and secondary schools. Musa felt it was a payback time, for him to carry over some of his father's responsibilities. He had to help educate his siblings. He had learnt and seen the value of education.

With these, Musa made up his mind to move to Nairobi where it was assumed that jobs were easy to come by. After all, he reasoned, he was not going to stay in the village with his enviable education tilling his father's land and leading the simple village life. It was not going to make much difference between him, a university graduate, and those who never saw an inside of a class. On the other hand, what kind of motivation would it create to the youngsters, who envied university education, if he had to idle around the village without a white collar job and basking on his past laurels?

He packed a few of his belongings in a bag in preparation for a new life in the city of Nairobi.

Chapter Three

To the east of Manga, where the sun, *omobaso*, first rises from every morning demonstrating its indomitable might, is Borabu village. A village that lies in an undulating landscape and covered with expansive green vegetative canopy. Several homes in Borabu were in a celebration mood. Their dreams and sacrifices had been rewarded. Four of the sons and daughters had graduated from the prestigious University of Nairobi. Judith, or simply Judy, was one of them. This was not their first crop. Every year, at least every home saw its sweats and sacrifices with a new graduate from a tertiary college. Many homes boasted of their sons and daughters in the city of Nairobi, Gusiiland and in other towns, harvesting the mushrooms Sakagwa foretold.

Judy Nyanchera Makosa's graduation ushered in a lot of joy and hope to her family. As the first born of Daudi and his wife Regina, her success was valued. Her parents perceived it to be an immediate catalyst to her siblings. They had invested greatly on her education. She schooled in the best and most expensive academies, and missed almost nothing in life. In a way, that investment had not disappointed them. As they got old, they reasoned Judy would be a launching pad for her siblings' career development. Nairobi was seen as a springboard for career development. And with the family's relocation from the city to Borabu settlement scheme upon Daudi's retirement from the civil service, Judy was their hope. The family had settled well in a relatively modern red-brick house built on a twenty acre farm. They were a well-to-do family, with a bungalow, electricity, a modern water borehole, and several grade cows; things any rural home would yearn for.

One evening, Judy's mother, Regina, called out for Judy to join her in their living room. It was a spacious room, fully furnished with expensive mahogany dining tables, two complete sets of red ease velvet sofas and a matching sizeable mahogany painted sideboard marooned onto the wall. The floor was adorned buttercream. On the wall, several family photographs, beautiful pictures, achievement certificates and trophies added life into the beauty of the room. Judy was seated outside the house building castles in the air and admiring the dilating landscape towards Manga. She had a lot of attachment with the ranges. Her grandmother, Marita, the daughter of Kiage and his wife Makosa had their home at Manga. Then, her dreams as a woman were held captive by one, Fredrick Musa of Manga. She had not seen him for some time and she felt the truth behind the saying, "absence makes the heart to grow fonder." She really longed to see him before she went back to Nairobi to look for employment.

"Makosa," Regina fondly called her again. "Your tea will go cold." Regina had prepared a cup of steaming tea and brought it to the table room.

The call caught Judy unaware. She quickly responded to her mother's call, "I am on my way mama," as she stood up to join her mother in the house.

In memory of her late grandmother, Makosa, Regina always called Judy by that name. To her, the name had more meaning than any other name. It evoked memories of her youth. It implied love, promises, commitment, patience, and above all, hope for a better future. In her stay with Makosa, Regina had learnt a lot from her, and seen her practice these virtues. She admired her effort and a back of steel, working tireless in her farm, weeding and cultivating. Without realizing, Makosa had become her role model. In Makosa, hard work, commitment, patience and love were epitomized and Regina had borrowed these virtues into her marriage. Though Judy was her mother's favourite child, Regina did not discriminate against her children. She always found time to spend and share with Judy as much as she did with the rest.

Judy strode in majestically, carrying with her the childish face she loved to wear. She assumed that her mother wanted an evening amidst the warmth of her daughter. This was not unusual. They always sat or strolled together in the village or marketplace spending hours chatting and laughing as if they were sisters.

Regina admired her long twisted steps: steps of a confident girl going to catch the moon. She was well groomed, beautiful and well fed with round cheeks. Any mother would congratulate herself for the work well done. Her smiles warmed her heart.

"A hot cup of tea will do the trick in an evening like this," Regina motioned her to the sofa. She poured steaming tea into Judy's cup as Judy sat next to her. She pulled her chair close to the table. It was a quiet evening with gentle dry breezes sending chills down the spine. The month of December, *esagati*, was a dry month with gentle breezes. She agreed with her mother that a cup of tea was very appropriate. Judy's siblings had gone to Girango to pay a visit to their grandparents, Marita and Chief Nyamweya. Daudi, Regina's husband, as usual had not arrived home. He was running his shop in the market centre and doubling as a church elder. So Judy naturally became her constant companion.

"When you were young, before your sisters and brothers were born, one kilogram of sugar could not last us a single day," Regina joked as she put sugar into Judy's cup.

"All children like sugar mama," she interjected defensively. She thought her mother was teasing her. "I'm not an exception."

"One minute," Regina calmly corrected her. "You're. You know my daughter, when you came into this world, we had many visitors from near and far who came to greet you," she stared at Judy in great admiration like a new birthday gift. "You're a special child you know; born to us in a special way. Your names are special too. Judith, Nyanchera and Makosa all have special meanings."

Judy watched her mother as she added two spoonful of sugar into her cup of tea and stirred it gently. She knew the hard moments her parents had gone through before she was born. She enjoyed the story being narrated to her again and again. It rekindled a picture of their struggles and determination. It reminded her that through these struggles she was finally born and had a special place in their hearts.

"Besides, you couldn't drink anything that didn't taste like honey," Regina reminded her in a joyous mood. Then she skillfully pushed the cup to Judy's side and continued with her story. She sipped her tea as she fumbled with her dress between her thighs. The briskness of the cup sent her basal glands active with warm saliva. "These days my daughter, many parents don't spend time with their children," she said as she placed her half-filled cup on a saucer. Judy listened intently as her mother spoke. "Parents are too busy with life while the children spend most of their formative stages in schools searching for knowledge."

Judy gave her an encouraging look to go on. "True mama," she agreed with her.

"And when they're finally out on their own, they have little preparation from the parents to meet the onerous challenges of life," Regina continued prophetically.

Judy put on a childish smile. She always felt like a child in the company of her mother. She felt much younger than she actually was. "My first experience in a boarding school mama was not a cup of tea," she interjected. "I lost a whole term crying and by the time I adjusted, I had lost a lot of weight."

"But I kept visiting you quite often," Regina equipped defensively.

"True mama," Judy concurred. "One visit made me look forward for another one. And by the second term when your visits became less frequent, I had already made friends with my classmates. Your constant encouragement to carry on was my greatest inspiration and strength."

As they chatted, Judy felt that her mother sounded relatively unusual. But it did not take long before Regina hit the nail on the head. As a mother she always found it necessary to prepare, or rather remind her daughter of the facts pertaining to matters of life. In doing this, she hoped that Judy would not embarrass her family or make mistakes which she would later regret and say, "oh, I wish I knew." As a caring and loving mother, she did not want to see her beloved daughter fall into those pitfalls of life and take blame for not preparing her well. Regina was aware that her daughter Judy, just like any other young girl could be prone to pitfalls that bring about emotional bruises, partly due to ignorance caused by lack of parental guidance. This was strengthened further by the fact that Judy had completed her college and was preparing to go to Nairobi in search of a job away from her mother's watchful eyes. This in itself, Regina noted, portended a great challenge to a young girl away from home and in a job market where opportunities had considerably dwindled even for those with a good education. Though Judy was now a mature woman and was of age and perhaps would soon bring a man home to present cows, in Regina's eyes, she was still a baby with little experience in life. Regina felt that it was her cardinal obligation to advise her daughter again and again on how to handle herself while in Nairobi especially in regards to relationships with the opposite sex. She knew that it was a mother's role to protect her children from the details of unhappy relationships and encounters, and from real, imagined or perceived dangers; especially Judy, who she considered her hope and a special token given to her at a time she needed her most.

"Makosa," Regina called Judy again. "There are issues I would like to remind you of."

Judy listened attentively as she nodded her head.

"I didn't go far in school, but I have many more years of experience than you. At twenty two, and out of college, you may be feeling old enough to do what you may want, and you probably want to take total responsibility of your life. And perhaps you even want to bring a few cows to this home?" Regina smiled at her last sentence. Some of Judy's age mates had already settled down in marriage with one or two children. The remark made Judy feel uneasy. However, Judy felt it was her mother's usual stab to her heart that never caused any bruises when it came to matters of the heart. It was her way of communicating issues. Hers was like the kicks of a horse that never hurt its young one. She smiled to herself quietly.

Regina was determined to be different from the mothers who never bothered to counsel their children. "You're now old enough to make wise decisions that will have a positive bearing on your life now and in the future. I believe good decisions are made from an informed choice. Unlike me, you've had a chance for an education and some good exposure. I did not get that chance. I got married when I was only in the last class of my primary school and that provided me with the first opportunity to step in Nairobi, the first town in my life. Then, I was a promising pupil in my class topping the list of the best performers. I had hoped to pass with flying colours and join one of the best girl schools, but it was never to be. Your father plucked me like unripe fruit. However, now, I don't regret it. There is no time, no room for regrets. It's too late. I see my successes in my children. I am lucky to have found a man like your father who has stood with me during the dark moments of my life, you know?"

Judy wondered what her mother was really driving to. She knew her as kind hearted and of great understanding.

She was quite patient and endeavoured never to bruise the feelings of others. She had in the past gone through tough experiences, which perhaps had assisted in shaping her character. When she shared an evening like this with her children, she always brought out her own experiences which worked well in her advisory role as a mother.

Regina's predisposition charms were inviting. She was generous to people. She always acted calm and composed even when life was not treating her well and had decided to take a turn for the worse. She avoided getting involved in petty village gossips which usually hurt the reputation of many village women and sometimes boiled into open conflicts. She preferred to digest her words before she uttered a word in public. These qualities and her intelligent posture added to her natural beauty that was still visible though age was slowly wearing it away, Regina remained respected by all in Borabu. Even with her little education, she was an opinion shaper of high integrity. She led the church choir and was a leader of many women groups in the village.

"Life can be gloomy, my daughter, without genuine friends. We make friends at all stages of life, each playing their own important role. Some are positive and others negative. That's why we must learn to choose friends wisely," Regina continued speaking calmly and in a relaxed manner. "Remember that not all that glitters is gold. Take time to observe before you rush to make conclusions or praises to something or someone. A handsome man isn't the colour of his skin, the sweet talk of his tongue, his eucalyptus height or the many papers to his credit. It's also in the beauty of his character. Good relationships can build while bad ones can definitely ruin."

Regina decided to revisit her past to suit her points as Judy sat pensively admiring her mother. "When I was young, the age of your sister Martha, our friends were our age mates who we shared a few childish games and other duties together. The girls' major duties were fetching water from the river downstream, fetching firewood from the forest and running errand for our parents and other elders. These duties did not allow us to interact very much or have enough time to concentrate in our academics. My aim was set on going to school, studying hard and acquiring the best education. I admired one of our madams, Judith, who you are named after, and who was always smartly dressed and spoke refined and fluent Queen's English. She always encouraged us to excel in our academic works if we ever dreamed of wanting to lead a decent life in the days to come," she stopped to sip her tea. She appeared distant.

"However, my daughter, my dreams were never to be," she remarked quietly. "*Nchera tiyana gotebia mogendi*, a road never informs a traveller what may be ahead. Our parents were always eager to see cows at home once a girl seemed to be of age for marriage," she laughed holding her mouth, with her stomach and sternum gyrating in rhythm. Judy joined her in encouragement. "With the marriage, the heavy loads of educational expenses were off-loaded, and instead replaced with abundant riches overnight from the dowries the girls fetched them." Again Regina and Judy took moments in a rib-cracking laughter in the imagination of this state of affair.

"One other factor that made parents want to marry girls off earlier was disappointment. Some girls just dropped out of school to elope after the parents had invested a lot in them. Their hearts were disparaged and broken. It was a disappointment," she repeated and Judy agreed. "Some were unfortunate victims of teenage pregnancies leading to premature termination of their education. Though these were rare occurrences, those unfortunate cases put their families to ridicule and shame. Girls who had babies before marriage did not attract suitors willing to negotiate for a high bride price. In a way this was a loss to the entire family. The saying, 'a house of many girls, is like a gourd that never dries of milk, and never experiences hunger,' was held with affection. And girls were truly a source of labour and wealth. With this understanding, some parents gave boys the first priority on education relegating the girls only to the second option. This is not happening now?" Regina posed authoritatively.

"It's a dead culture mama as parents are now realizing the potential of girls and the contributions they make once they are educated," Judy answered. "Perhaps ignorance and perceived lack of appropriate opportunities for educated girls contributed to that."

"Others thought that a girl's place was in the kitchen cooking food, or in maternity bringing babies into being, while others felt that an educated woman would not find a husband. Who would want his daughter to be a spinster just because of a cause not well comprehended?" Regina added, "Who would want to touch that woman? With a breached skin and an expanded head embracing alien thinking?" Some people could be heard saying. Some people wrongly thought that with education, women would never accept to be told by their men let alone respect them."

"It's a bad notion mama," Judy noted. "It must change and the rights of women respected."

"A lot has already changed now compared to that time," Regina observed. "So when your father snatched me from my home to the city, this appeared to have done the trick. My father on learning of my new status as somebody's wife, he did not even boil or demand me back to complete my school. Not that he wanted to get rid of me or he did not love me. No. As his first born daughter, my father almost adored me. As a child, he could not go to bed without kissing my cheeks or calling me '*omboto*,' the one with round cheeks. I don't have reason enough to blame him for his belated action. It was fashionable then not to worry so much about girls' future. It was said that their future would be taken care by their husbands. Traditionally, men went out to hunt while women remained at home to take care of the home and children. This role transformed men into almost sole breadwinners. My father demanded cows almost immediately. I was worth the world to him and indeed my worth fetched him twelve zebu cows, a bull and a goat. Wasn't that great?" Regina had infectious sense of humour.

"Mama, your worth could have been higher with a better education," Judy insisted. "Today you could be like that madam teacher you used to envy or even in a position of influence, perhaps making decisions that affect the lives of many people in society."

"You are right Makosa," she continued, "as young girls, we were very much disciplined," Regina emphasized. "We did not entertain boys who wanted to harass or disturb us." Regina wore a shy smile as she narrated her youthful experience. "No! Boys waited for us on the way as we went to fetch water, firewood or while on errands. They disturbed us," she said amidst laughter. "They proposed, you know, but we brushed them aside like the hurricane wind. But when your father appeared on the scene and proposed, I got confused and found myself yielding and promising. It was unlike me who had made a reputation all over the place of being a no-nonsense, tough and disciplined girl: daughter of Chief Nyamweya. My reputation spread far and wide. Every parent told their daughters, 'see, and be like Regina, the daughter of the Chief Nyamweya.' But it was like your father had cast a spell on me." Mother and daughter laughed together shyly. "My father was happy that after all, I was going to fetch him some reasonable wealth," she posed. "He was a young handsome man. I had seen him a couple of times before on my way to my grandmother's place." Regina tried to recall in details the encounter as she unconsciously acted younger. "When he first approached me, I ignored him. Truly! Oh yes he was an enigma of a kind. For then there were aspects of his qualities I could not understand. I didn't know whether he loved me. I thought he was only teasing me or taking advantage of me; a mere village girl. He was older than me by almost six years. Yes, I knew he was working in the city but that alone added more fear in me. What on earth would an elite city dweller want to do with a girl of a remote village other than take advantage of her? Weren't there better looking girls in the city? Those who worked in Nairobi were thought to have a lot of money, to be fun-loving with a mentality of despise for the rural folks and their simple inexpensive lifestyle. It was said that their visits to their rural homes were just a mere fulfillment of their obligation and as part of rural tourism. They were more exposed to life beyond the horizon of the rural people's reach. There were better girls in the city who had a taste for life. These reinforced my fears. What was he after from a local village girl who did not have any city mannerisms, let alone a language to effectively communicate? So I ignored him, and when he appeared to press on, I called him names. I wanted him to leave me alone. I was too young to be teased. On top of all that, I wanted to fulfill my academic dreams," Regina recounted with overwhelming nostalgia.

"If one wants to catch a fish, and fails to catch it with a hook, then one can try a net. It was in one such encounter that I finally found myself in his knight net. I had called him all the insults I knew so that he could stop disturbing me, but as I turned to go, after thinking that the battle was finally won, in a way, his prayers were answered. I knocked my right toe against a boulder which was firmly half buried unnoticed in the sand." Regina put a painful grimace on her face as she pointed to Judy the toe that was hurt. Still there was a visible scar that had refused to fade away with age.

Judy bent over as she examined it, "it must have been very painful mama."

"Leave it," Regina's face was turned into a mask of contortion. "I slipped in great pain and fell down headlong spilling all the millet in a basket I had carried on my head to my grandmother, Makosa. Though, I had abused and insulted him, your father came over, held my hand and helped me up. I cried like a little baby wanting to be nursed by its mother."

"I'm sorry mama," Judy tried to comfort her.

"At that time I could not refuse a helping hand from even the devil," she beamed with smiles of relief as she said this. "He took his clean white handkerchief from his trouser pocket, cleaned my bleeding toe and bandaged it. He then proceeded to salvage some of the spilt millet into the basket. Only half of it was gathered as most of it was mixed with sand. He carried the basket all the way to my grandmother's place without uttering a word as I limped behind him like a wounded wild cat with my entire body aching in excruciating pain."

"He really acted like a good samaritan," Judy added.

"He was indeed a gentleman," Regina concurred. "When he left me, I started re-examining this man who had ostensibly bestowed upon me kindness that I did not deserve. Yes, I had known him for some time. He had shown a lot of interest in me before and now his actions spoke louder and demonstrated to me that he was dependable and he respected me. He was a gentleman by deeds. I was slowly drawn to him over time by the warmth of his kind heart, the charms of his soft spoken and appealing words and in a way, his urbane mannerism and status. His genuine care and concern too won me over, transforming my stubborn feeling to strong love for Daudi. I was simply the Biblical Goliath defeated by the little David in a war he was confident of winning. With this encounter I must admit that I lost terribly. I lost my desire for education and my stubborn spirit that had reigned in me to say no to Daudi's advances. I found myself longing to see him again and again," she posed with a light chuckle. "Later, when he proposed to marry me, it was a belated request. I did not summon my head to consider the proposal. I found myself yielding with ado. To make a long story short, my daughter, that's how I met and married your father," she sunk onto the sofa with a heavy sigh.

Judy looked at her mother expecting more. She had been captivated and entertained by her mother's narration: a story teller of a kind.

Regina had not concluded her story. This time she started with less ebb and less liveliness that permeated strong feelings of sadness and dissatisfaction with life, which Judy easily detected. "When I joined your father in Nairobi, I was the envy of every girl. I was happy to have a chance to stay in the city where I did not have to go to the river downstream to fetch water, or to the forest to look for firewood and then load it on my head and bring it all the way home. If I wanted water, I just turned the tub on and water flowed out. For the first time I experienced the comfort of electricity. I no longer had to strain my eyes in the smoky filled hut. I used an electric cooker to prepare meals, showered in hot baths, and had the opportunity to watch television and sleep in a comfortable bed. Above all, I was happy to have a husband who showered me with love. But then, these were not all that I wanted in life to be happy. I was a woman too with a woman desire. My dreams were not very different from any other young woman. In my dreams, I longed for a complete family. A family with children for who our sweat would not be in vain, whose presence would warm up the house and signify our sense of belonging and our dignity, whose images would be our pictures on the walls, who would illuminate our house when it was dark, to provide a shoulder to lean on when life reaches the evening, and who could take the stool, the spear and shield of their father to carry on with the mantle when the creator takes the moments." Regina narrated as if she was reciting a poem. "But mine was not a happy stretch of an even path. Years came and went like an estuary of a swollen river. Time passed in a snail's speed." Regina's voice started to waiver. When Judy looked at her in the eyes, a silver sheet of tears covered her corneas.

All this time Judy had been keenly listening to her mother. Never had she seen her behave like this. One of her mother's strength was her ability to withstand adversity. She was courageous and a source of comfort and strength to many. Judy thought quickly to comfort her, but Regina had already summoned her inner strength and courage in time. The silver sheet of tears on her corneas was meticulously transformed into an icon of beauty and radiance, wisdom and intelligence, perseverance and courage. With a wide smile on her face, she said what pained her most, "ten years into my marriage, when I had almost given up, you came into this world. You are the opener and the blessing of my womb, the hope of our future."

Judy listened attentively almost forgetting what had happened a while ago. She was perturbed by the pain her mother went through for her cause. She felt sorry for her though she knew that her mother was taking her role as a parent in guiding her too. The lessons she could derive from this evening discussion were many and relevant to her life.

By the end of their talk, Regina felt she had imparted and equipped her daughter to face life's challenges from an informed position.

The sun was setting beyond the horizon. The cows had returned home from the field and were crying for attention. Regina and Judy stood to wind up the day's work. As usual, Regina started singing her favourite song which always found full admiration from Judy. It sent warm celestial feelings down her spine in an evening like this:

1. *Ogende kaa omwana oyo iga ogende kaa*
   Ogende kaa omwana oyo iga ogende kaa
   Onteberie baba, baba ominto tanyeba

2. *Ogende kaa omwana oyo iga ogende kaa*
   Ogende kaa omwana oyo iga ogende kaa
   Onteberie tata, tata ominto tanyeba
3. *Naki aranyebe baba ominto onyiborete?*
   Naki aranyebe tata ominto onyiborete?
   Naki baranyebe baibori bane banyiborete?

1. Go home my child go home
   Go home my child go home
   Tell my mother not to forget me
2. Go home my child go home
   Go home my child go home
   Tell my father not to forget me
3. But how can she forget me, my mother who bore me?
   But how can he forget me, my father who bore me?
   But how can they forget me, my parents who bore me?

And as she sang, Regina felt and saw herself younger beside her father, Chief Nyamweya and her own mother, Marita, the daughter of Kiage of Manga village. Regina imagined herself beside her mother. Marita was singing the same song in the evening as she prepared millet and sorghum into a straw-woven basket and telling her, "*baba ondane*, the beloveth of my own womb, take this millet to my mother, Makosa. Take it and tell her not to forget me, her daughter."

With each verse she sang, the song became livelier and fuller. The yellow evening sun shone with dimmed brightness, weakened vigour and intensity. It mimicked its last golden rays with unfeigned reluctance as if saying, "fare thee well, farewell till we meet again," before finally setting to the west of Manga behind the hills of Bosongo.

Chapter Four

Musa's encounter with Judy Nyanchera Makosa continually rang in his mind. It was one of the most beautiful things that he couldn't forget in a hurry. It was his first year and fifth day at the university as a fresher. The first year students had congregated in the main campus hall for the popular fresher's ball organized by the university to welcome them. A jubilant mood engulfed the hall packed with new students. Their faces were lit up with the new experiences and excitement of being on campus. To add to these, they were still excited that they had emerged at the top of the previous year's Kenya Certificate of Secondary Education (K.C.S.E), which had earned them places in this prestigious institution of higher learning. The K.C.S.E exam had been competitive with only less than ten percent of the students qualifying to join the public universities. Musa was excited when he caught a girl smiling at him. It was a familiar face with bright, gentle, intelligent eyes: Eyes that can easily convince a thief to come out of his hide-out. Inside he felt calm and an intense longing for her companionship that evening. He had unknowingly and compulsively been smiling at her, and incidentally Judy was just considerately returning his smile. He acknowledged her smile with a broader smile and flick of an eye, then turned his head and stared at the vice-chancellor as he eloquently gave his opening speech. But he was not paying attention to the chancellor's speech. His mind was divided between the speech and the familiar girl. She had the most beautiful face he had noticed that evening and remained glued there in admiration. Then slowly he recalled. He had seen her before in Manga. She was the great-grand-daughter of elder Kiage of Manga. Judy.

Judy was a frequent visitor to Manga on school holidays. Musa had seen her there before. Often Regina, her mother, the daughter of Marita brought her children to visit her grandfather, elder Kiage. It is in Manga where Regina had spent her early life with her grandmother, Makosa, the wife of Kiage, fetching firewood and water for her. She had made friends there and always recalled how with her friends they played games at the ranges and swam in the waters of Manga stream and smeared mud onto each other. Manga was more her home than Girango. Like all women, she equipped, "*mokung'u tanya kweba ase geting'e na ase rorera*, a woman does not forget two places: the place of her umbilical cord and the place of her anklet." Elder Kiage and late Makosa were the parents of Marita the mother to Regina. And in her visit, Regina and her children looked meticulous in their urbane mannerisms and dressing compared to the simple village life where children dressed in tatters and walked bare feet. They were an attraction and people came to see, greet and admire them.

In their orientation around the campus earlier that week, they had met again several times but he had not taken note of her. To him Judy was just another fresher who appeared sophisticated and exuded good nature and confidence.

Judith Nyanchera Makosa or simply Judy was born naturally beautiful. There was no doubt about that. She did not require any make-up to change or enhance her superb looks. Her beauty was ingrained and enhanced by her striking personality and her grooming. Her wit, umber radiance, well developed mannerism, and unassuming character added to her charms. She was fairly slender, fair in complexion and medium in height. Her teeth were milk white, sizeable and well set in her mouth. Her face was round, matching well with her wasp-like waist, a slightly protruding back. Her legs fleshy, fatty and almost round like two ripe hybrid bananas. One could easily notice Judy's beauty as she walked or laughed confidently almost oblivious of her surroundings.

Musa stole another glance at her. He felt inside an urge to talk to her. She was an old acquaintance he had played with in the waters of Manga stream. They had jumped in the streams together with other boys and girls of Girango and Manga, throwing and smearing mud onto each other, laughing and chuckling. "Children being children," as the elders said, "did not see any barrier between them."

The orientation period had been uneventful. They had not attended any lecture. Much time had been spent on learning the university's administrative structure and registration of units. The students spent the evenings hours socializing in various groups of old acquaintances comparing notes and experiences, or having fun, especially those from same schools or homes.

The dance was finally opened to the students by the Vice-Chancellor who was the main guest for the occasion. The live band played the most popular hits of the time which found full admiration from the students. Many students took to the floor to dance while others just sat on their seats to enjoy the beats of the music and watch the occasion in admiration. The beats of the heavy musical instruments burst into the air appealingly. Judy sat on her chair enjoying the sensational beats and the baritone voice of the lead singer. It bellowed a smooth but deafening voice. When the rumba beats were played, she found them too appealing to be glued on her seat. Like everybody else, she took to the floor. She stole gentle steps with the rumba beats. It was on the dance floor where she met Musa who courageously synchronized his movements with hers. She willingly danced to the rhythm alongside him. They danced until the middle of the night enjoying every bit of it. When the band packed off from the stage, they were left sweating but discerning more. They retreated to their respective residence halls to sleep. This was the longest encounter with the opposite sex for both of them. The encounter left Musa with awkward feelings towards Judy that he could not clearly understand. It was a genesis of their journey for better things to come. Musa escorted her to her hostel as they chattered and revisited Manga. No doubt, Judy was sociable. Musa secretly admired every bit of her. When he retired to his room to sleep that night, the experience with Judy did not allow him a wink. He stayed awake for a long time recounting the moments he had spent with her. He just wanted to meet her again.

The next Monday, Judy and Musa found themselves in the same lecture room. Now they were not strangers. Both had enrolled for a degree in B.A Economics. With each encounter in the lecture rooms, and along the corridors, Musa found himself wanting to meet Judy more and more. Her sociable nature won her many friends and admirers. Their uninvited eyes unconsciously followed her, all the way admiring her until she disappeared at a corner leaving their minds following her from behind in wishful admiration. Judy was equally aware of her subtle charms and she loved it. Inside, she remained calm and she wanted to be humble and respectable always wanting to take after her mother, Regina who by her nature, had won many hearts in the village of Borabu, her rural home.

In many occasions, Musa and Judy sat side by side in the lecture rooms and did assignments together. These opportunities served to bring them closer. They visited each other frequently in their hostels. Their friendship grew in leaps and bounds. They found themselves spending part of the weekends together chatting or going for outings and doing assignments. They talked about Manga and Borabu. Judy's great-grandmother, Makosa was a product of Manga, Musa's village, but several homes away. Makosa's daughter Marita got married to Chief Nyamweya of Girango just across the ridge of Manga. Having spent part of her early life with her grandmother, Makosa, Regina always had fond memories of Manga. And she always talked about the village remembering her friends and the games she played with them as she grew up. Borabu had literally taken cows to Girango in exchange for Regina when she was married to Daudi. And if Musa was to marry Judy, Manga was only to return the cows that had come from Girango which Chief Nyamweya, the father of Regina paid to Manga as bride price when he married Marita. This would cement the relationships and build bridges.

By the time the first semester was coming to an end, Judy and Musa had become inseparable. First, they were drawn to each other by the shared past as children who had met as youngsters and played together, and then by natural forces they could not resist. To bridge the gap created by the holidays, they shared their experiences through long love poems pouring out their loneliness to each other. And by the time the holidays were coming to an end, the longing to see each other had become intense and pronounced. But Judy's love for Musa remained mysterious. She could be too assertive and indifferent; never committal.

As they came to the end of their degree, Musa felt that his love for Judy had matured. He was confident that he had met the girl of his dreams and hoped to marry her at the right time. He dreamed that after he got a job he would settle down with Judy and live happily ever after like the fairy tale Cinderella.

Regardless of having the same roots, Judy and Musa were different in many ways. Judy was mysterious and unique in her birth and in her upbringing. She was brought up in the city of Nairobi in a relatively well-to-do home. Her father was a retired senior civil servant who, at his highest, commanded a lot of influence. In contrast, Musa's background was a simple village life: a village that had shunned education and modern trends for too long. A village that had struggled to retain what their forefathers held dear. He had grown up a simple village boy struggling against many odds. He walked to and from school bare footed, he tethered cows and goats, and he lead a simple village life.

At one time, Musa's father, Mogaka, had operated a butchery business in their village. The business had done relatively well until the dreaded foot and mouth disease struck the whole district, killing most of the animals. It was a catastrophe which took people by surprise and took long to forget. Homes were left without cows and the children were literally deprived of milk. Musa was just a small boy back then. Mogaka was forced to close down the business due to shortage of animals for slaughter. Then he joined the rest of his family in tilling his five-acre piece of land; the only remaining spring of livelihood for his polygamous family.

The land could have been bigger, but Musa's grandfather had many wives. They were six, each with a special name. The sixth one was simply referred to as a maid to the first wife. He had paid several cows as dowry for the first two wives. The next two were gifts for his outstanding musical entertainment during ceremonial occasions. He was known to play his *obokano,* lyre with both eyes closed. The last two, he married them from the cows of his trade, as a renowned medicine-man. When the land was shared out amongst the wives and then the sons, each inherited a small piece. Mogaka got five acres from his mother.

During good days of business, Mogaka always came home in the evening with a package of food for his family. Like all men in the village, he frequented the local *busaa* clubs where he could drench himself with beer before coming home. Having taken enough, he could stagger home in the evening or middle of the night with his package in two separate nylon bags singing merrily and momentarily stopping to haul abuses at his supposed enemies daring them to a physical confrontation of which he was always sure and confident of winning. Often word came that Mogaka had been seen lying by the pathway drunk. His wives and children took turns to fetch him home. Sometimes he could praise himself for being the cleverest and bravest man in the whole village of Manga. Clever, in that he had children in school, and brave because he could walk in the night without fear of witches, thieves and wild animals. In the process, he would stagger, slip and drop his loads and rush to pick them. By the time he reached home, the packages were usually dirty. Then he would survey the homes with greater assertiveness wanting to know whether the cows had been milked, the shamba had been tilt, and all the children had come home from their various duties.   He would move from the first house to the second wobbling with such amazing tenacity shouting and unleashing terror at the slightest provocation.   Every member of the family feared and respected him and went into hiding. The house where he spent the night, Mogaka always delivered the package with the lion share of meat among others. Once he entered the house and was quiet, his children and wives could resurface from their hiding places to resume their duties. They laughed and imitated how Mogaka had wobbled and talked. His actions were no big deal to them. He was their authority and he was merely exercising it.

The next morning Mogaka always woke up calm and friendly to all, assuming nothing had happened the previous evening. He could call his children by the special names he had for them. "My father, my uncle, here is a pencil. My daughter, my aunt, my grandmother, here is a rubber." He would put his hands in the pockets of his trade mark long overcoats and remove several pencils, rubbers and exercise books. "Here, go to school and study. My land is small and you have little to inherit from me. My flock has diminished. Go to school, excel and buy your own land and cows." Then he would share with his wives how he had drank with his friends the previous day and incidentally blamed beer for all his misconduct promising to stop all together. However, he never stopped. A day or two, he would repeat what he had done previously. People would say, *"nyang'ere ndotung'i, na mori yaye rotung'i, etakogwa eng'ina n'ekogwa ise,* a calf takes the characteristics of its parents, *nyang'ere,* and if it does not resemble the mother, it resembles the father."* Mogaka had taken after his father. It was said that his head did not want beer. It was too weak even for a cup of *busaa,* a local brew made from fermented flour and yeast. Unfortunately, his habit impacted negatively on some of his children. Some ignorantly picked up his behaviour as the acceptable way of life as they matured. Consequently, they did not take their education seriously and this again negatively impacted in the overall alleviation of village conditions.

In spite of this, Mogaka was regarded with respect as the head of his family. His behaviour was not strange. Most men in the village asserted their presence that way. Although Mogaka's two wives were overtly rivaling for him, it was not seen as strange. He was their man, and it was considered traditionally normal for women married to one man to rival over one grinding stone. One of his wives could be heard singing in an evening, *"moibori omino, moibori omino, ere n'ekerecha kere enyasi. Mosuko ndakwe, acharara irongo areta obori bonga inkomba,* ones co-wife is a devil lurking in a wall. When I die, she rushed to my ceiling to fetch my clean millet. He would advise them, *"Mokungu o'siko moino kae Bosibori ensio yaye nero moibori omino agosera,* the woman of the other house, let co-wife have her grinding stone as it is the only one she has."

In the village of Manga, Christmas was the most envied occasion, especially by the youth. Though many villagers had somewhat accepted Christianity, it was the only occasion when most children wore new clothes, usually second hand or new school uniforms. It was the only occasion when bread and doughnuts, *mandazi* were eaten and tea with sugar taken *ad-libitum.* The other days, children were forbidden delicacies for they would make them rude or not grow fast enough. The truth was that these delicacies, as they were termed, were beyond reach. They were simply too unaffordable and were seen as a preserve for the well-to-do.

The festivals could go on for days extending beyond New Year's. They alternated from one home to the other until all the homes were visited. It created cordial ties. One had to make peace with a neighbour they had differed. During this period, virtually no work was done, apart from milking cows. Children were forbidden from taking beer though by the evening, most of them could be seen drunk or smelling of beer acquired from *busaa* remnants, known as *emeseke* in beer pots stored under granaries. Some mischievous children made frantic effort to steal undiluted beer from the houses. No one bothered to ask them. Once drunk, children could sing choruses in praise of Christmas, their teachers or any known great person. At the height of the celebration, the old folks already intoxicated from beer also sang and danced to *obokano.* During these occasions, boys could have the opportunity to dance and flirt with the village girls in the dark night outside. Only that the elders were not supposed to know. But then, every girl knew that her respect and future rested on how pure she remained in order to attract the most suitable suitor.

This background, which Musa grew up in contrasted sharply with Judy's urban set-up where she had been born and brought up and received the best things in life.

Chapter Five

The night bus slowly pulled to a halt at Nairobi country bus. It had cruised half the night from Manga to Nairobi. The street lights were on, partially illuminating the streets of Nairobi. But, it was too early for the passengers to alight as Nairobi was said to harbour many criminals. Thugs were said to lurk in dark corners ready to strike at unsuspecting passengers. They sprang into existence with tenacity at the sight of a human shadow. Musa looked at his wrist watch. It was around four o'clock in the morning. It had been a long journey from Manga to Nairobi. The city was lifeless, quiet and streets deserted with only a vehicle or two passing after some time. He pulled out his huge black bag containing some of his belongings, mainly his clothes, placed it on the seat of the bus and rested his head. Then he closed his eyes and tried to sleep.

Nairobi wasn't going to be a heaven of peace. He knew this so well. He had set his mind to face the new challenges in this enormously big and tricky place as a job seeker. With no source of livelihood, no one to hold his hand, he only hoped that soon lady luck would open the doors and his dreams would come true. He knew he was joining thousands of young graduates in the job market and he had only to rely on luck and perseverance to survive. The competition was stiff, a situation found in the jungle where only the fittest animals survive. He had faced challenges in the past, and he had emerged through them without being shattered. He owed it to his parents and teachers who encouraged him. Against all odds his parents managed to pay his school fees. His determination and hard work saw him conquer his fears. This realization gave him a flicker of hope. He was prepared to plunge more than ever before to survive the challenges.

Nairobi was the one place where many youths thought jobs were readily available, especially when armed with good education and someone to act as an intermediary in the job market. He had an impressive degree, yes, but he did not have anyone to 'hold his hand'. That was a great disadvantage. He did not have anywhere to stay, or finances to sustain himself as he took the plunge, but a friend from across the ridge, Girango back in Manga, had promised him shelter for a time.

Peter had been an anchor to many job seekers and knew Musa would be coming from up-country. That may have temporarily solved one of his problems. But for how long was he to be sheltered? He did not have an answer. Peter was married and stayed in a two-roomed house in the sprawling Dandora estate. He had studied up to form four and came to Nairobi to look for a job. Luckily, he was employed as a clerk in the ministry of transport after several years of doing menial work. To cut on cost, he had rented a two-room house in the lower class estate from where he commuted daily to his place of work. He was known in the village of Manga and most of the young men coming to Nairobi to look for jobs always found a home in his house. He was a kind hearted man, and having seen the advantage of education, he always encouraged young people to read harder, to do professional courses and seek professional jobs where possible. This personal drive had often made him accommodate many people in his house, even though the costs of living were pressing on him harder. Nevertheless, he had to shoulder the village misfortunes. That was the way to uplift it. That one had earned him a good name in the villages of Manga and Girango.

When the sun started surging up in quick succession with its yellow rays illuminating the city, Musa alighted from the bus. The vehicles had already started commuting and the streets were alive with people walking in all directions. He was now certain that it was safer to walk in the streets without being mugged. Stories of people who had been mugged were frequently told, and he had to take precaution not fall victim. He walked to the bus stop where he took a *matatu* to Dandora Estate. The *matatu* moved at a snail's speed in the heavy file of traffic jam stopping now and again to pick up more passengers. Finally, when he arrived at Dandora, he got off the bus and walked a half a kilometre to Peter's house. There were two more form four school leavers staying with him. They were all job seekers. His wife had moved home to ease the burden of city life.

Being a Sunday, Peter was still in bed when Musa arrived. The door was partially closed. Musa tapped the door softly, and then opened it when he heard a welcoming voice. Peter was his age mate and a friend. They had faced the knife the same day and had uncountable experiences together. Peter was peeping from the inner room half covered with a towel when Musa entered the room.

"Welcome brother. You have made it so early," Peter smiled from the room as he extended his right hand. They shook hands in prolonged embrace.

"Its fine with me," Musa responded as he shook Peter's hand. It was a warm hand having been in bed. "Everyone at home is fine. They all send their greetings."

"Thank you. How are uncle and aunt doing?" Peter inquired.

"Except for father, who has a slight cough, everyone is alright. People are busy preparing their gardens for planting."

"The rains may come for planting." Peter welcomed Musa with the kindness of a brother. Though he was slightly older than Musa, it was only a matter of months apart. He was born in the month of December, *esagati*, when crops had ripened and there were festivities in the village, while Musa was born in the month of April, *rigwata*, the following year when a mysterious wind from the lake caused heavy down pour filling the rivers and streams. Peter's bulky body betrayed his real age. He appeared much older than he was. He was a polite man with rather keen intelligent eyes that had been sharpened further by the life of the city. And indeed, he was intelligent.

Peter and Musa had grown up together. As youngsters they had a lot in common. They played games together assembling and flying kites in the ranges, herded cows in the ranges together and went to school together. With other friends, sometimes they fought over ridges supremacy. Now it was water under the bridge. They were initiated into manhood under the same tree using the same knife. This past childhood experiences had thickened their bonds. They called one another *yaa*, meaning age mate.

"They are complaining that you haven't gone to see them and you have not sent them anything for a long time," Musa continued. "I met Angela, your darling, and she wonders whether you married her or Nairobi," he informed jokingly.

"True *yaa*, I was home three months ago. I haven't gone back to see them," Peter was apologetic. "I miss Angela, my children and my kinsmen, but yaa, you may know Nairobi. Money, time and distance home have put a wedge between us. It is like our pockets have holes." Peter talked half smiling. "The cost of living leaves me with nothing to spare, yet they always need money from me." He had gotten used to their complaints. "One time, it's about money, the other time it's about me not having visited them. I love them. I wish they could understand my situation: that I am operating on a tight budget. Finances are scarce nowadays and the demand is too much," he tried to reason out. "Food, transport, clothing, *harambees,* donations in a spirit of pulling together and name them. By the end of it, I remain with no coin."

"You haven't gone to visits them for a long time. They say you've forgotten them and you've been swallowed by the city life," Musa justified their complaint smiling.

"I was at home last Christmas. Our people at home always believe that once you're in Nairobi you have a lot of money. Anyway I'll arrange to travel home before they 'forget my face' as they put it." Peter joked in laughter.

"Three months is too long. *Yaa*. Angela could be too lonely. You know, she is young and needs your company and she must be coming first in your life."

"If finances could allow, I would have invited Angela to live here with me." Peter was in a distant voice, "perhaps with that, she would realize the fullness of marriage."

"That is what marriage was meant to be. Together," Musa tried to reason, "for good and for bad. Struggling together, crying and laughing together heals the heart. Loneliness can drive a good marriage apart."

"I met aunt last season and she wants you to marry now that you've completed college," Peter interjected with a feeble sarcastic smile playing on his lips. "That is what your mother always says," he emphasized, "You are of age and she wonders what you are waiting for."

"We're age mates, separated in birth by only months. I only completed college the other day. I need time first. After all, life is not all about marriage. And for a young man like me of the modern times, I should rather take my time," Musa acted younger as he completed his last sentence. "In any case, good girls are rare these days."

They shared the jokes in a prolonged laughter. Peter agreed with him but not without a tease. "I'll get a good one for you in the city."

Musa felt that he was not alone. After having been disappointed by Jacinta, Peter did not give up the hope of meeting a young beautiful lady to marry. Months after coming to Nairobi, she had not waited to fulfill her promises. She walked out of Peter's life and eloped with her former boyfriend who paid cows to her father immediately. Peter's heart sunk. He felt that he had lost part of himself. He pleaded with her, but when he realized that it was all over, he had to seek solace elsewhere. He worked hard in his job, enrolled in a Certified Public Accountants (CPA) class and this occupied his mind, momentarily. Though wounds healed, three years down the line he had not yet met another charming lady to think about and fill the void. Angela appeared from nowhere one morning at a wedding. Before he knew it, he was head over heels in love with her. Three months later, they were husband and wife. A year later she relocated home to ease the pressure of city life. Three years after that, they had seen the blessings of their marriage: two children, a girl and a boy who he adored.

There were two beds in the room. One right at the corner and the other ran across. The open space served as a living room and at night a mattress was laid for visitors to sleep. A square metre of space was left where there were a few kitchen utensils and a gasoline stove. "The two gentlemen who live with me have gone job hunting. I expect them in the evening," Peter informed. "They have been here for two months now but luck has not knocked on their side. I admire their endurance and determination. They do any job that comes their way."

Musa surveyed the room. It was small and squeezed. Three people living in it and now him. He wondered, "I have also come for the same," he swallowed warm saliva, "I don't know whether you'll be at home with me too. But I need your direction to start," he remarked uneasily.

Peter knew that another responsibility had been added to him. "Be at home with yourself yaa. You and I are like brothers of the same womb. We have grown up and done many things together. The two gentlemen I stay with here are hardly related to me, but we have had a past together. Our fathers grew up together and are friends. So we are friends too. Friends come handy at times of need. This is my simple philosophy of life. It is the philosophy of our fathers and our people in the villages."

"I knew you would give a shoulder the moment I stepped into the house. I look forward to getting a job soon, maybe very soon so that I can help my parents ease their load, realize my sweat and map out a future," Musa remarked politely as he surveyed the rustic ceiling and pealing walls.

"The unemployment situation in the city right now is terrible without one to hold your hand. You have to try and keep on trying without giving up," Peter advised him. "After all, a man has to struggle to succeed in all he does. Struggling may tire or wear out one, but it does not kill. It hardens. Likewise we live hoping that tomorrow will be better than today. When the sun goes down in the evening, we don't wake up the next day to the previous day. Have a peace of mind, settle down and relax. Where I can, I shall help. Where I cannot then goodness and mercy is with you," he gave him his assurance Musa.

Musa felt relieved with that assurance. A little hope built inside him, but only for a moment. He knew the struggle had only just begun.

Chapter Six

Two years elapsed slowly and uneventfully after Musa came to the city to seek employment. The job market was saturated with many young graduates from all sorts of colleges and universities, and others from high schools competing for available vacancies. Some of the job seekers were his former college mates and remarkably, one was Stella Achieng. Having been past acquaintances, Stella turned out to be his constant companion in the streets of Nairobi. They moved together from office to office in search of a job. They shared the days' experiences and these made life bearable. They were not alone. Many were going through the same experiences. With this realization, a portion of hope built in him with an assurance that a day will break in with a tinge of luck. Somehow, these shared moments with Stella unconsciously pulled them together.

Days had turned into weeks and finally two years. Feelings of disillusion and despair started cropping up. Every step Musa made in his endeavour to secure a job was regrettably frustrating. "No job! No vacancy! At the moment we have no suitable vacancy!" These posters screamed at the gates and responses from his prospective employers followed in the same manner. They were discouraging and required a strong personality to maintain one's sanity. Somehow, through prayers, hope and determination, he managed to move on.

The writings on the state of the economy of Kenya were on the walls. In the recent past, the nation's economy had performed dismally. It had failed to impress or attract new investment or donor funding. Business interests were collapsing and a few remaining were relocating to other countries were the cost of production was lower and hence offered better returns to investments. The remaining local companies and state corporations were carrying out their operations from a weak financial position. The scenario therefore deprived the nation opportunities for employment. Even those organizations thought to be on sound financial position were ideally troubled and were struggling, doing everything possible to survive. Some were merging operations, integrating their functions and services, embracing new technology and ideas to make them more responsive to the challenges posed by the changed and competitive business environment. The years that followed saw hundreds of employees declared redundant from the civil service, state corporations and the private sector that were under disguise of the donor prescribed retrenchment, liberalization and privatization programs. These programs were ideally lauded from some quarters as the only best alternatives to stimulate the ailing economy back to sound state. Lo! The results proved to be quite painful for the many young graduates. The doors of employment were painfully slammed to the youth. Ironically, the extra labour force released in these programs joined the labour market to compete for the few available opportunities thus creating more competition. Even then, it was rumoured and whispered that if one was looking for a job, one could quicken his or her steps if one knew someone of influence, the top management, or 'scratched' the back of the people who mattered. These realizations were disturbing, and discouraging. The trickle-down effect was, "why persevere all the way through school only not to secure employment in the right way."

The crime rate spiraled up. Young disillusioned youth unable to get employment did all sorts of things. Some started small *jua kali* businesses. Others threw their academic papers and took any available job. It was no surprise to see a graduate with a degree joining city council as a sweeper or a guard. Others joined a trail of politician sto heckle and disturb rallies of the opponent with promises of employment, while others took into drugs and anything that would offer livelihood and ameliorate their stressful situations. Musa was not left behind. He had to move with the times.

Musa swore not to give up. He always tried his luck in any suitable advertisement and then prayed for God's intervention. In some occasions he was honoured with an interview. Armed with his certificates, he always felt confident that the time had finally come. His determination to conquer and earn for himself a livelihood was overt. However, the post interview replies were usually negative. It was not a secret that the successful candidates were those who were well connected to the cream of the organization. It was known that one could not be employed in such and such organizations unless one parted with "tea" to the people who mattered, or had a 'good go-between'. So what about the press advertisement and the well set interviews? They were a formality. It was like wearing on a clean outfit on a dirty body, applying cosmetics on an unwashed face. Simply, the interviews were a public image enhancement gimmick to assure the public that all was well when it was not.

Peter consoled him. Musa secured a casual job in the industrial area through a friend. It had nothing to do with his degree. He had to earn a living against all odds, adjust with the reality of life and move on. The job involved loading and unloading heavy goods into and out of train wagons. His strong muscles ached with the heavy load. He had to do the job anyway as he had learnt the hard way to adapt to the situation and that nothing good came that easily. He put away all his pride and education but wore a brave face. However, the wages paid on a daily basis were barely minimal to afford a fare and a decent lunch. So, he walked to and back from work, and avoided lunches.

He took the job with the all the enthusiasm. He worked hard to impress the bosses. The work was heavy, tiresome, requiring little skills, but it was the only alternative at hand. He accepted it as it was: The noise in the factory without any earmuffs, inhaling dust without nose-masks, and the crude way of doing it on bare hands. Yet, for one to come across such a job, one must have had a 'heavy weight go-between'. But then the job lasted as long as the 'go-between' remained relevant. Within a short while, Musa was back to the streets to map out the next move. He had no go-between to negotiate for his re-engagement.

With the little money he had made, he resulted to hawking biscuits at the country bus. Every traveller with a baby was a considered a good customer. He had to sweet-talk them to buy his biscuits. He called the biscuits all praises. They were sweet cakes, *mchezo wa meno, and malaika*, name them. Sometimes he closed the day with enough sales to pay fare to and from the estate and leave some money for a rainy day. Sometimes the goods were not moving, so he had to spend what he had saved previously. The marginal profit was minimal. Some hawkers sold their goods below wholesale price. That was when it became evident that many goods were smuggled in to evade tax while others were ill gotten.

Business was not all that easy. He had to contend with an unfamiliar territory. Established hawkers did not take his entrance into the business kindly. One almost picked a fight with him over a customer. Rude customers were the order of the day. But he learnt to deal with them. Some people perceived hawking as a crime and looked down upon them. Their dignity was compromised. Then there were frequent battles with the city council *askaris* (guards) leaving a trail of damaged goods and injuries. Hawking went to the late hours of the night. He had to content with the risk of being mugged at his work place or on his way home.

The little earnings he made were quite valuable. His

shoes needed replacement, the pairs of trousers were already torn, and only a single shirt was remaining. These could be replaced with second hand clothes, *mitumba,* which were relatively cheaper and available.

In the evening, Musa would resign to Peter's house and focus to his past and see his ambitions crumble before his face. Before him, were so many hurdles to jump over or circumvent. The success of it depended on several factors beyond his reach: the family background, the poor national economy, the right connection to the circles that mattered, and to an extent, the money to buy his way to employment. As he went through school, he perceived education to be the key to success. Everybody in the village saw it that way. They saw it as breast milk they had all along denied their children, and an escape route from their misgivings. Times had changed greatly. It was no secret that many triumphant men and women had gone through it. He had considered himself lucky to have climbed that far up the ladder of education. Armed with this he had dreamed of big things. A rewarding job befitting his relentless struggle, a sleek car to his credit, a descent house in the upper market, a comforting wife and children who did not cry for the basic necessities, and something to spare for the education and well-being of his extended family back at home in Manga. He yearned to be a role model to the young people at home who would see him through a reflector mirror and work hard in their studies for a rewarding education. Further, he had a desire to open up Manga, to embrace the changing trends as an inevitable chance to develop and be counted among the surrounding villages. He felt convicted and locked in this poor and sorry state he was in. He felt like a spider caught up in a blind spiral web, in recirculation.

Chapter Seven

Judy and Musa had gone their separate ways after completion of their university education. As they parted in tears, they promised each other to keep in touch.

"I'll forever remember the shared moments and miss you dearly," Judy had said.

"I shall keep you updated," Musa had promised. "And the Lord be with you till we meet again."

"When we meet, we shall become dudes and allow you to bring cows to Borabu," she remarked jokingly.

"And I shall. On the alter before an enviable congregation, I shall take my vows," he replied, "to the delight of our parents, kinsmen and friends."

These were the parting shots as they said good-bye at the country bus. And for some time before the ember extinguished, they called and wrote to each other poems expressing their lonely feelings and experiences. They communicated in long love letters in an earnest endeavour, pouring out their feelings and their struggles. Phones rang at the middle of the night. However, the ember waned with time. The saying "out of sight, out of mind" held water. With time, communication started to wane. It could take weeks before one placed a call or wrote an exciting poem. Then all of a sudden Judy went offline. All his many letters and calls went unanswered, leaving Musa guessing. He could not understand what had happen to his love. "Perhaps it is the distance apart," he thought. "Perhaps she did not receive my poems, letter or her phone must have been misplaced." Unknown to Musa, the challenges of being a job seeker had frantically glared before Judy. With the changing trends, Judy had developed divergent views to life and realized new expectations. Judy had rediscovered herself. She dreamt of money and a comfortable life. Unlike before, love was not the priority. She was not meant to fly the same direction as Musa. No. she discerned more than that. Life had taught her a few lessons. A man is more of a man if his pockets are worthy looking at twice, she had concluded.

As a girl, Judy never missed going to church. She would tell her mother, "Mum today it is my turn to pray for food." And her mother would allow her to pray. She would pray as if she was possessed with Holy Spirit. On weekends she would assist her mother to prepare her siblings for church. Attending church service was her way of life. She would sing in the church and recite coral verses to the merriment of the congregation. The congregation would ask one another, "Whose daughter is this?" and would say, "she is such a blessing."

Their father, Daudi, always accompanied them to church. This boasted their morale. They never missed church functions like baptisms, confirmations or crusades. Her zealous mother nurtured Judy's faith and at a tender age of twelve, Judy was one of the most active members of the children's church choir. She was subsequently accepted into the baptism class, baptized and confirmed. She remained an active member of the church throughout her childhood and throughout her university years.

Judy's beauty and strict manner stirred and gave young men heartaches. Some felt intimidated by her and avoided her. To others, it was a source of what she termed as unwarranted disturbances. She avoided groups of girls who she saw or were perceived as spoilt. In short, she was a girl every parent in Manga pointed at with applause and wanted his or her children to emulate. They would say, "look my child, I will like you to be like Judy, Regina's daughter." Nevertheless as a mother, Regina always wisely and constantly guided Judy on the right path to follow and she had not disappointed her.

Fatima, Ombati's house girl, was not as educated as Judy. She had dropped out of school after primary education then went to Nairobi to stay with her aunt. Fatima's aunt was a hairdresser and owned a medium salon in the city centre. It was relatively modern, attracting a number of clients especially on weekends. When business was prime she had always assisted her aunt without pay, but when the customer were fewer, she stayed at home or assisted in her bar where she mingled with male patrons. These encounters gave her a lot of exposure for a young mind, and it is here she met Calvin. Having been brought up by a single mother who was a barmaid, she did not see anything wrong to working in a bar. With time she felt that she needed a constant and assured source of income of her own. She tried to look for a job but her level of education was limiting. After a few trials with a house help agencies, she was employed by Judy's uncle, Ombati.

While Judy stayed in Nairobi to look for employment, she stayed with her uncle, Ombati. She shared a room with Fatima, who was talkative and assertive. It was hard to ignore her and so, Judy and Fatima quickly struck a rapport.

Fatima was a tall, well-built and attractive girl with utter feminine features. Even with her limited education, she had an overpowering influence over Judy. Her thorough exposure to life had given her several real experiences which she always narrated to Judy every time an opportunity arose. She had largely grown up on her own with no guidance at all. Her mother was never at home and when she came late at night from a bar where she was working as a barmaid, she was always drunk and immediately fell dead asleep. Her parents had separated when she was too young to remember, and she had grown up with no father figure around.

When Fatima was in class five, her elderly grandmother took her in her care when her mother went to jail for being in possession of illicit brew, *changaa*. With her little old energy, there was not much for them to eat. She allowed Fatima to roam freely soliciting for food from kind neighbours. This equally gave her an early exposure that was not favourable for a young girl.

"Judy," Fatima was in a jovial mood one evening when she called her. "I've something good for you tonight, but I can't tell you now."

Judy was anxious. She wanted to know what Fatima had for her. They had become close friends, sharing a lot of stories and fun as the job market had become elusive and frustrating. Since her coming to Nairobi to stay with her uncle in South B, Fatima had become Judy's companion, always spending a lot of hours talking, laughing and doing domestic chores together.

"You are killing me with curiosity. Please tell me now." Judy pleaded.

"No. Not now. Just be patient. Patience pays, you know? I'll tell you later in the evening. It is a good plan this time," Fatima insisted.

"Four is already evening," Judy insisted.

"Lack of patience killed the hyena by eating its own intestines, and hurry hurry has no blessings," Fatima urged on.

"And the early bird catches the worm," Judy jokingly teased her.

"If you can't wait, then alright. Alright then!" said Fatima, "since you've insisted, I'll let the cat out of the bag, but on condition that you'll not let me down this time round."

Judy was anxious, "I'll listen. I'll try."

"Tonight Calvin is taking me out to Tourist Resort Club. He is willing to have you in our company. Say you'll come with us."

Judy was silent for a while. She had never been to a club and she had never contemplated going there. "No Fatima. I won't accompany you. You know me. My faith! Then what if uncle comes to know of it?" she reasoned.

"Today you will. It won't hurt your faith. What sin would you be committing by accompanying us? I also have some faith, but I go. All those who go to clubs have their faith too." Fatima commanded convincingly. "I'll take care of all your needs," she toned authoritatively.

"Mmm… I've never been to a disco or a bar or spent a night out," Judy pressed on. "You know I'm a Christian and saved."

"Tonight you will be in one," Fatima insisted commanding. "Imagine how boring it is being here all day long. We definitely need a break and a change. That is not sinning," Fatima insisted further. "Look here Judy. You're now a grown woman. You need to explore the world and at least enjoy the nice parts of your youth. They say if one misses opportunity to explore life at a young age, one wants to make discoveries at an old age. Tonight, you shall dance, eat, drink and be here before they are up. Nobody will know. After all, tomorrow is a weekend, you can afford to relax then," Fatima tried to sound convincing.

Fatima had always nagged her on this issue, but Judy had vehemently and politely refused to join her. This time she felt terribly torn inside. She was saved and committed to her Christian faith. Her parents and everyone else regarded her highly. She did not want to frustrate this trust. Further, she feared her uncle for his strictness and did not want to offend him and his wife Hellena. His wife was even stricter. It was not out of malice, but they wanted to protect her just like her mother had done from the many dangers and troubles they perceived young ladies like her could get into in the city. In addition, she had Musa who she did not want to offend. Yet, she did not want to hurt Fatima who was so close to her now. She was equally bored, lonely and frustrated with dreams of a job crumbling before her. Then, the urge to explore the world started burning inside. "After all it isn't a sin to go out," she reasoned. "Fatima could be right."

At the same time she felt mature and responsible for her own life. After all it was her life, she thought. She felt she needed some freedom to enjoy herself and explore the world away from the home ground, where her age mates passed weekends, laughed freely, danced and enjoyed themselves. Every time Fatima had gone out with Calvin, she came back rejuvenated and with new and interesting experiences to narrate. "It had been nice there dancing to the latest *Lingala*, reggae or blue, ohangla beats and so on."

Fatima's boyfriend lived in the neighbourhood. She could sneak out at night through the back door when everybody was asleep to meet Calvin. She would be back in the wee hours of the morning before anybody was up and tap their bedroom window softly. Judy would wake up to open the door for her. Fatima brought packed roasted chicken and snacks for Judy. They would eat them as they talked and laughed in low tones between the sheets on how her outing had been exciting. Fatima would narrate how she enjoyed the dancing and how her boyfriend showered her with love. This would naturally spill into Judy's heart leaving her with jealousy and loneliness that sometimes she felt needed to be filled. She was young and a woman too.

A voice seemed to whisper to her, "No, Judy no. You shouldn't allow yourself to be get influenced blindly by Fatima. You shouldn't go where you have never been. You're being misled. Stand by your guts. You've always done it. Don't betray those who have great hopes for you. Don't betray your faith." Another would tell her convincingly, "Listen Judy! You are a grown woman and no longer a mother's kid. Go out like Fatima and other ladies and enjoy yourself. After all, life is about happiness." The second voice was more instructive and convincing, like Fatima. She felt weak and confused.

Judy thought for a while. She was a bit scared and bit courageous. Scared of what? Courageous of what? The answer lay in the consequences of her decision. She was torn within herself. She stared up at the ceiling in deep thought, looking for an answer. In whichever way she looked at it, she stood to gain or lose. She reasoned. She walked to the bedroom and lay down on her back while Fatima continued washing the utensils in the kitchen.

The saying, "if one keeps company of a thief one will eventually steal," held true. Darkness was beginning to fill the room. Judy got up from the bed and walked lazily to the kitchen where Fatima was busy preparing an early evening meal for the family. Fatima did not see her coming.

"What time are we going?" Judy almost whispered. She had made up her mind.

Fatima turned and looked at Judy with her eyes wide open. May be, she wasn't expecting what she heard. Judy appeared calm but with a resolve. "What time are we going, I ask?" she asked again.

That was the last thing she expected from Judy. For a while Fatima was taken aback, but she realized she had to give an answer. Then she smiled at her and replied, "at ten, after they have gone to bed. Prepare yourself. Put on the best outfit you can find. You can borrow a pair of my jeans, perfume yourself and paint your lips red. It is romantic that way," Fatima answered instructively and excitedly. She had won a battle she least expected to win.

Judy walked back to their bedroom with her hands folded on her chest to do the best she could in anticipation. They were buying time. Once their uncle and aunt were safely in bed the pair would sneak out as planned to the Tourist Resort Club.

Chapter Eight

Tourist Resort Club was a heap of activities that night. There was music, dancing and eating roasted meat, *nyama choma*. There were many patrons: young and old. Young ladies and men of Judy's age whiled away their moments zonked in intoxication. Fatima danced rhythmically with Calvin to the rumba beats. The dance floor was packed with disco lights shining in pre-determined patterns. Judy sat at a strategic corner to have a clear glimpse of the events. She tried to make herself comfortable. She wondered if this was real or a dream. It was her first time in a bar. She sipped her soda as she watched people dance almost bare, drink beer, smoke, tease one another and overtly misbehave. It was like she was watching a movie or in a deep dream. Yet it was a reality and it was hers.

Fatima came to where Judy was seated. She held her hand and gently pulled her from her seat to the dance floor and tried to assist her in moving with the beat. One after the other, Judy swayed her hips, twisted her hands and neck with the heavy beats of percussion from the background. She embraced Fatima and danced freely. She realized that she could be flexible and with each move, she regained her confidence till she was sure she was dancing beautifully.

The walls, the tables, the chairs and the counter were all decorated mahogany or made of mahogany timber with several decorations and designs. The umber, the elegance perhaps drew the patrons. While she could hardly make a coin, patrons appeared to care less, contented and spent as if they had all the money in the world and the world was coming to an end.

As the music played, Judy started to feel part of the crowd. The initial fear melted away. She no longer felt guilty. It was here on the dance floor that Judy met Richard Morgans, from the United Kingdom.

Fatima walked out and came with a white man of middle age. She danced with him as Judy and Calvin mingled and danced. Finally, the four were dancing together in a circle to *mugithi,* a kikuyu music. When the circle was broken, the white man synchronized his movements with Judy's. Somehow, Judy responded to his moves and danced with him to the blues percolating from the walls.

"I'm Richard," he whispered into her ear amidst the loud music. "Richard Morgans is my name," he reaffirmed with a bellowed voice.

"Mine is Judy," she replied.

"Aah, that is a beautiful name," Richard teased her.

Judy was now relaxed and like everybody else enjoying herself. She felt calm. Perhaps Fatima was right to have insisted that they have an evening out, she thought.

"I'm from GB," Richard informed her further.

"You mean Great Britain?"

"Right," he affirmed. "I'm a tourist."

Richard held Judy's hand gently and led her to an empty table at the farthest corner, next to where Fatima and Calvin had taken seats. Though she felt a little uneasy, she followed him like a sheep to the slaughter. They sat opposite each other. His kind and gentle smile disarmed her. Richard beckoned a waiter and ordered a bottle of vodka and two sodas. Meanwhile, he engaged her in conversation. They talked of Kenya and Britain. And with this Judy had no doubt she was in the right company. The waiter served them with their order. Richard paid him and he left. Richard filled Judy's glass with a mixture of vodka and soda and an ice cube. Then he filled his with the same stuff, toasted cheers then invited her for the drink. When Richard pushed the glass of vodka mixed with soda, Judy did not resist. She wanted to feel how others felt when they take beer. She took the glass and gave cheers to Richard; she sipped a mouthful of its contents and let it down her throat with her eyes closed tightly. It was bitter like raw herbs. She sipped several times and almost immediately started feeling its warming effect. Heat, excitement and dizziness, the vodka had started to take effect.

Fatima watched the events from her seat with parted breath. She could hardly believe that the Judy she knew could sit with a stranger and drink alcohol. She walked to where Judy was seated. She was already zonked. She whispered to Judy's ear, "that is a good catch," then walked to the dance floor swinging her hips to the beats of the music. Judy smiled at the joke. She had learnt to figuratively swallow Fatima's naked sarcasm.

"I've been to Kenya several times," Richard explained amidst sips of vodka. "And every time it is an exciting experience. I've grown to love this beautiful country with good sceneries, games, entertainment and sociable people. It has lot of opportunities for business too."

Judy listened keenly as the effect of vodka was taking a toll on her, giving a mixture of a nauseating and refreshing effect she could not describe. She was feeling strange things moving all over her body.

"I sell pharmaceutical products in the UK," Richard continued.

"I completed my college and I'm now prospecting for a job," Judy informed him.

They talked, drank and ate roasted meat as the night wore away. Richard was very friendly, generous and informed. Judy felt that she had found a friend, someone to share some moments of fun with: To drift from the disappointment of being unable to get a job and the stresses of life. She told him about herself, about her family and her ambitions in life. For that moment everything went on just the way she wanted. Finally, Richard pulled her to himself. She was already drunk. She weakly fell on his shoulder. Richard caressed her. He held her tightly. Judy felt a mixture of excitement and fear. She felt guilty. "But what about Musa? Was she not offending her mother, and God?" she thought. But the courses of events were too fast to reverse and the solution was not handy. Richard kissed her fleshy round cheeks. She felt a strange calmness all over her body and an overpowering urge she was not going to resist. While she enjoyed a lot that night, Judy could not fathom the course her life had taken. And as they say, "one does not taste honey once, he tastes it twice." Judy wanted more of what she had experienced.

When it was approaching four o'clock, Fatima came for Judy and announced, "Judy, It's time to leave or else we will betray ourselves. I hope you had fun with your friend."

"I mustn't deny. I've no reason to deny," she answered.

Judy excused herself to go home and they made plans to meet again. Richard escorted her outside the club. As she boarded a taxi, he squeezed ten dollar bills into her palm. Judy was grateful. The taxi dropped them near their house, and then they tiptoed fast to their room through the back door. The rest of the family was asleep and nobody had a clue that the two did not spend the night in the house.

Fatima and Judy went straight to bed. Fatima fell dead asleep almost immediately while Judy lay lazily in bed on her back staring at the ceiling. She took out the money from her hind pocket and stared at each dollar. They were beautiful brand new US dollar notes. She counted them one by one up to a hundred. Then she returned them back into the same pocket as she thought of how lucky she had been that night with little strain and in a shot while she had made ksh 80,000 at the prevailing exchange rates. Manna had dropped from heaven. Perhaps, she reasoned, Richard was the hope of her life. He had promised her a lot, only if she proved cooperative.

In the wee hours, Judy fell asleep. Before morning broke, she had dreamed thrice: twice about the US dollars and once about Richard. When she woke up late in the morning she was feeling lazy and tired. She walked to the dressing mirror and looked at her bloodshot eyes. She stretched her body left and right as her muscles ached. She conceded she had had a night and half that she was not going to forget in hurry. She felt time was moving fast, and she needed to move along with it as Fatima always told her, or else she was going to be left miles behind the world and she would never catch up no matter how hard she tried.

Again that night Judy did not spend in her uncle's house. She waited until everybody was asleep, then she slipped out quietly to meet Richard at the Tourist Resort Club. Fatima watched over her until she safely disappeared into the dim street. There were still a number of people moving up and down from and to town. She took the late *matatu* to the city centre, alighted and then walked to Tourist Resort Club where Richard patiently waited for her and had laid for her a red carpet.

Richard hugged her and tossed her up like a toy. He ordered roast chicken and vodka for her. For the first time, Judy drank till she blacked out. That night, she lost her virginity to Richard. There was a little blood in the lower sheet, but Judy took it as a proof to her woman-hood. At five o'clock, Richard drove Judy back to the house. She walked fast to their bedroom and tapped on the window. Fatima woke up and opened the door for her. With these experiences, Judy had engaged a forward gear and there was no stopping. She equipped to Fatima, "honey is sweet, but no matter how sweet, it cannot match my Richard and his dollars."

Chapter Nine

Ombati and his wife Hellena knew that their house girl, Fatima was not an infallible girl. No she wasn't. They had hired her from a reputable domestic services agency in town that took reliability for any eventuality from their house girls. They saw her as a human being disadvantaged by her poor background, with the earthly weaknesses and emotions to take care of. They had collected her from the wreckage of her life where she lived in oblivion. They had taken her in and endeavoured to guide her through the path of life. They were a strict couple in the matters of life, always having a watchful eye on all activities around their home. They were careful to watch how Fatima related with their children. Like any other loving parents who spent most of their day at work, they wanted the best out of them, and they were aware that a responsible house girl could help shape their children's futures from their formative stages. Fatima spent more time with their children than they did.

Fatima's commitment to duty was commendable. She created an impact. The children adored her. They called her auntie. She called them "my children." She had quick legs, a back of steel and a tongue sweetened with honey. She tended the kitchen garden like a professional agriculturist, worked hard in the kitchen, did the laundry, mopped the house clean and rightfully organized it to everybody's satisfaction. She had done this effortlessly and ungrudgingly for two years. Her day started early. She prepared breakfast for the family, fed them, warmed bath water, bathed the children and prepared them for school. She then took them to school and picked them up in the evening.

Fatima had not gone far in school. Her poor background could simply not permit her this opportunity. But everyone agreed that had she gone far, she was to surmount mountains. Fatima had no room for regrets. Too much water had already passed under the bridge. She had accepted her situation and now wanted to take advantage of whatever came her way. She was a rather carefree person, discreet with an innocent childish face which made her appear naïve. But Fatima was not a green horn. Hardship in the slums had led her to nasty experiences in her childhood.

The greatest source of attachment between Fatima and Ombati's family was the way she socialized and related with the children. It was commendable. She kept them immaculately clean, fed them to their satisfaction and arranged them on the table to read. Fatima could also receive visitors and telephone messages like a qualified secretary. The family was happy with her. They had no reason to worry about their coming home late so long as Fatima was there. And when they were at home early they were usually tired and exhausted from the laborious day. They were always chasing business or developing their career paths. Ombati was a successful accountant while Hellena a marketing executive.

Hellena pitied Fatima when she painfully narrated to her, her difficult slum life. Her experiences were full of poignancy: often lacking, going to bed on an empty stomach, braving a leaking roof, trudging on filthy paths and contending with embarrassing morals. And with this understanding, Hellena and her husband wanted the best for Fatima, perhaps a total transformation in her life for the better. They prayed that her future would take a different turn, perhaps changing fortunes for the better. She was too good a girl to undergo eventual torment not of her own making. Hellena felt that Fatima was an indispensable girl in their family and hoped that when the right time came, she would send her off to her matrimonial home with a token of appreciation for the good work she had rendered to the family.

Fatima did not return from her usual weekend off. Nobody knew where she had gone and what had happened to her. Hellena was devastated. One week turned into two, and then a month passed without a trace of her. Judy could only guess that Fatima had eloped with Calvin, her boyfriend from Eastlands.

Judy knew Fatima was expecting the moment she found her vomiting every morning. Fatima was apprehensive when the doctor said politely and jokingly that she was going to be 'bringing' a king to the world when one morning she decided to go for medical checkup. She had been feeling sick and tired every morning she woke up. She did not think much of it, and blamed it on having too much work on her hands.

Fatima knew the consequences of the new turn of events. She was going to be a mother, something she was not prepared for. She was not going to continue living and working at the Ombati's home. How was she going to handle the shame? And with no job, how would she feed the little king the doctor had said was on the way? When she finally confided her situation to Judy, she only consoled her. Yet, she wasn't so sure of Calvin who, after graduating from a diploma college, joined the underground drug dealings when he could not secure a job. However, she had to face him and plead with him to bear the responsibility. A wounded cow has no choice than limp home.

So, that weekend she walked to the barely empty room that was Calvin's dwelling in Eastland and informed him of the little 'king' that was on the way. Calvin characteristically puffed several cigars. He was in a somber state. He had nothing to say. Though he had on several occasions wanted to marry Fatima when moments were right, she had always declined his offer. She had considered herself too young to take up the hectic responsibility of running a home, and being called someone's wife. She had not fully had fun with her youth. But the opportunity had forcefully come along. She had no choice.

Calvin loved Fatima. She required emotional support at that moment, he reasoned. Now with her 'legs broken,' she required a home to settle and call her own. It did not matter how it looked. Whether in the worst of the slums or on the top of an ice cap mountain, it did not matter. He had been brought up by a single mother in a slum. He did not have the privilege of knowing his father and the pain was still there. The ridicule from other children calling him "fatherless" whenever they wanted to hurt him was too much. This had made him resolve that his children should grow in an environment with their father. They needed to feel loved in a complete family. Abortion never crossed his mind. With all these considerations, Fatima had lost and a golden opportunity had knocked on his door. He had won the battle. Battles are won by brave and determined soldiers but generals get credits and decorations. In this case Fatima was a general and Calvin, a foot soldier.

Calvin puffed his last cigarette moving uneasily from one point of the house to the other. Yes, he loved Fatima. But with the new reality, no job and no money, what kind of family would he bring up? Won't she be disappointed and call it a day when the harsh truth come to bite? But birds live in nests, work in no one's shamba, yet they eat and sing every day. He was living in hiding since police knew that he peddled prohibited narcotic drugs. So he was not making money any more. However, he reasoned, he had to give it a try. "You are at liberty to do as you wish," he finally found his words.

Two weeks later Fatima collected her belongings from Ombati's house and moved in with Calvin, to the dismay of the Ombati family. To Judy, Fatima had won a justified battle and this increased her desire for more freedom.

Judy was in an elated mood. In less than a month, she had made five hundred thousand Kenyan shillings. This was not even near her wildest dreams. She walked to the wardrobe, opened it and removed the notes stacked in a big khaki envelope. She put the envelope on the bed and proceeded to empty its contents onto the bed. She was all alone in the bedroom. Brown currency notes half covered the bed. She started counting the notes one by one, arranging them methodically in a bundle of fifty thousand shillings each. The exercise took almost an hour of deep concentration. All these were her earnings as a courier and salesgirl, delivering drug consignments from Richard's hotel to established customers in the city, collecting their payments for onward transmissions to Richard; a job she did dutifully. Judy owed Richard a lot of gratitude for offering her this lucrative job. For only two months she was thinking of things she could only dream about.

The drugs she delivered to customers were usually packed into small neat cartons which were carefully sealed and perfumed. She hired taxis, loaded the drugs into the vehicle single-handedly or with the help of Richard and Calvin who was his salesman too. The customers usually paid her money in cash. At a time, she could carry thousands of shillings which she brought to Richard in the hotel. In most occasions she worked at late hours or early morning hours when the traffic was heavy. Richard explained that these were the right times to meet the customers. However, she noted that the business was highly secretive and involved a circle of few, regular and wealthy customers who she could meet at pre-arranged places. There was no official office from where the business was conducted. These did not bother her so long as she received her dues.

Richard paid her well. She would accompany him to the five star hotels and clubs in the late hours of the night. Her schedule started very early and ended late at night.

Already this had started raising eyebrows and complaints at home. She did not want this to continue. Judy felt she needed her freedom to transact her business. She wanted more freedom and time to spend with Richard. The only option at hand was to move out of her uncle's house and away from the watchful and questioning eyes of her aunt. Now that she had a job and money she could convince them that staying on her own was inevitable. Richard had asked her to rent her own house which could equally serve as their temporary store for drugs in transit to the customers. He was going to foot the rent for her.

Richard portrayed compulsive or obsessive interest in Judy. Understandably, she was beautiful. He had no way of hiding his feelings towards her. He adored her, called her sweet nicknames, tossed her up each time, and took her to new places. He could literally get sick if a day passed without seeing her, so he said. She was an asset. Her elegance concealed his illegal business. He was a very special person to her too. He appeared concerned and caring about her welfare. His enlightenment about life generally was commendable. He had travelled to this city and that country. He had simply uncorked the bottle, pulled Judy out of it and opened her ignorant eyes to the joys of the world, the world of business, money and romance.

That same evening Judy informed her uncle, Ombati, of how difficult it had become to operate from the house given her demanding job. She requested to be allowed to moved out and rent a house nearer to the city centre where she worked. After a brief thought, Ombati acceded to her,request but not without a piece of advice. "Don't let us down. The city is a tricky place for young women. Stay safe." With their approval Judy had all the freedom in her own house in the upper market of Runda.

Chapter Ten

The afternoon was hot with the bright blue sky appearing distantly. The air was dusty, almost smoky. Musa had walked most of the morning hours from one office to another. He had refined his ways of identifying prospective employers and had devised strategies to enable him go through the tightest security spot checks to meet the bosses and present his certificates with the hope of securing employment. A few tips had become obvious: know the name of a boss and fake a relation, or say you come from the same rural home. The evils of tribalism, nepotism, sectionalism and 'something small' were real. It was easy to earn the benefit of doubt and be allowed into the premises where he would request a job as if he was asking God for a chance into heaven. But two years down the line, lady luck had not yet knocked on his door. He was still jobless in a city where life was extremely hard and circumstances could easily corrupt good morals. Breaking through was not like a chick breaking the membrane of an egg shell to wriggle out of the shell to a new life. *Jua kali,* the informal employment sector, was an option but it was easier said than done. It needed a kick off capital, good-wills, entrepreneurship and he would have to be prepared to foot kickbacks, bear frustrations, stiff competitions and the city council *askaris* (guards).

Musa had sworn not to return to the village of Manga. How would the people of Manga look at him? A university graduate, their supposed epitome of hope. How would they perceive education? Is it worth the sacrifice of a poor parent to invest in an unrewarding education? Had education lost its lustre and reward? Would the youth who had started to envy education, especially university education which they associated with prestige, a rewarding job and successes, envy it anymore? Was it necessary to burn the midnight oils only not to realize the fruits of the course? He was the very first fruit of education from his village and he felt cheated and demoralized. With these disturbing questions that lingered with no ready answers, he felt weak. He had no reason to return to the village to prove that education was no longer that important and rewarding. These reinforced his decision to add more vigour in search for a job. He remembered one saying, "one day it shall break well from the east, *Mocha*, and set down well to the west, *Bosongo*." Despair would not be the answer. It would break the village, crumble the little progress it had made, and kill the morale of the youth. It would crumble his personal ambitions, and the great hope his family had placed on him. He remembered when the whole village gathered at his home after his graduation and sang in praise of him. Indeed, they had looked at him with great hope and in him had seen a 'morning star'. They had seen a lot of meaning in education. When a hunter goes to the jungle to hunt, he leaves the people waiting for him to come with a game. A good hunter therefore must learn to use his spear well. He recalled the many evenings when food was not available. The entire family would go to bed with empty stomachs. The next morning, the children would wake up early with rumbling stomachs to warm themselves around the hearth with a fire that simmered weakly. It kept them warm. Men and women worked hard to till the land. When the seasons were favourable, the crops grew healthier and stronger from the deep, rich, dark soils to provide sufficient food. The people would rejoice and always remembered to give thanks to their god, *engoro*. The seasons were always followed with festivities. Initiation of young boys and girls to adulthood, and marriage ceremonies followed. The ceremonies were important, but by the end of them all, the resources were depleted and the village was back to square one, lacking in food and essentials.

Musa felt hungry and tired. A lunch was not an option, but a luxury. He walked slowly toward the expansive Uhuru Park. There were many people seated in small groups, others moving up and down, while others bathed in the afternoon sun or hid from it under canopies of the umbrella trees. Several Christian groups sang choruses in praise of God while others preached at various points. They received ready audiences from people who came to 'eat' the spiritual lunch. He joined one group of gospel singers who had pulled a sizeable crowd. For some time he filled himself with the 'spiritual lunch' as he waited for Stella. This was their meeting point. Stella had become more than a friend after Judy disappeared.

He walked from the singers to an open space next to the ceremonial dais. He lay down on his back on an appealingly green grass. He stared up at the sky. The hot rays of the sun burned through the hazy tissues of the small distant white clouds. It ruthlessly radiated its silver rays with vigour and intensity. The sun slowly passed the slow moving clouds. He wondered how Galileo, the ancient Greek philosopher, came up with the theory that the sun was actually stationary and the earth revolved round it, when in abstract the sun was in motion. Yet, he could not convince the rulers of the time, who like him, looked up and stared at it rising in the morning and going down below the horizon in the evening. No wonder he contravened their teachings of the time. He earned for himself the most dreadful reward.

He laid waiting for Stella. He had loved her and still wasn't sure whether he didn't. Perhaps, Judy had disappeared because of his joblessness which had put him in an awkward state, an unsalable figure, he was convinced. And Judy was ashamed of him. "But then, why shouldn't she?" he wondered loudly. He took a small pocket mirror he usually carried in his pocket and looked at his reflection. Though haggard and troubled inwardly, he was presentable with short spatial beards on his face and an emerging moustache. Stella praised him every time they met. He was educated at least with a degree. But Judy had walked away when he needed her most to comfort him and tell him sorry for the way the world was treating him, for the joblessness, the hunger and the pain of unfulfilled hopes. Education had been his hope for a better life. And Judy had been another one too. But that was water under the bridge.

He closed his eyes and fell asleep. In his nap, he saw Stella coming. But it was only a dream. He watched her walk with all the elegance. She was beautiful, very beautiful indeed. He surveyed her up and down then from bottom up. She was glamorously beautiful. That day he planned to walk her around the park, hand in hand, tell her what he had never told her, that he loved her more than the fairy tale character Cinderella, that she was more beautiful than most queens. Then in whisper propose to her.

Slowly, he started seeing flash backs of his earlier days. Stella had been in his life since he was young. She was the young girl who captured his heart the first time in the village when he wallowed in innocence. It was her he noticed first as his eyes of innocence first opened to appreciate the inherent difference between a woman and a man. That was in primary school.

Stella Achieng was his desk mate in primary school. Though she was the youngest girl in class, she had the brain of a computer. She was the brightest pupil. She scored the highest marks in almost all the subjects beating all the boy and girls hands down. This made her a darling to teachers whose praises worked to motivate her. Her industry was the envy of many pupils in class. Some boys particularly did not like her. The mathematics teacher always compared them with her. Stella was excellent while they were weak.

Musa and Stella shared textbooks and walked the same way home every evening only that he walked a little ahead. They shared other things too. If he was in the list of noise makers, Stella's name came second after his. So they were punished together, but the teachers were always keen to remind them that they were only driving away the mistakes and making butter and bread for them.

Stella was not mean. She was always willing to share the knowledge she had with the other pupils. If she had a new story book that no one had in class, she would not hide it under her desk like some pupils did. She shared it. This won her many friends too who wanted to study harder.

By the time they were in final class, Stella was growing into a young woman. Her breasts had started forming standing sharply on her chest; her legs filling in with more flesh, and her burst becoming more rounded than in previous years. She had entered the challenging stage of adolescence like all the pupils in class. It was at the same time Musa's voice had grown hoarse one morning. His body was more muscular. It was at this time that his eyes opened and knew that Stella was a girl and he was a boy. He naturally found himself feeling an urge to be close to her and spend time together.

In the evening after school, Stella and Musa always walked home together with other pupils. One day, he recalled, they walked home playing *onyuro*, a game for boys and girls similar to volleyball, but scoring means to hit the rival who tries to evade the ball. She reached home later than usual. This did not go well with her mother. She was angry. She immediately reprimanded Stella for arriving home late from school. In the evening after school, she had to fetch water from the river and do her homework. This meant she had to be home early.

Stella was the beacon of hope for her family and it was the mother's role to ensure she was well trained and protected from the many dangers young girls could get into.

That was on a Friday. But then his admiration for Stella was intense.

The next Monday the teacher moved Stella from his desk and replaced her with the class prefect. This almost put a stop to their constant chats, which often resulted in being put on the list of noise makers. Stella made a point of rushing home immediately after school. She never walked slowly like before. Maybe she had been warned against being late by her mother, and as an obedient girl she was, she preferred to obey her, he thought. But every time they played games, she always gave him an appreciative smile.

The schools closed the following week after their Kenya Certificate of Primary Education (K.C.P.E). That was the last time he saw her until three years later when they had gone for cultural festival in Kisumu. He was in Maseno while she had passed with flying colours to secure a place at the prestigious Lugulu Girls High School. Mobile phone technology hadn't penetrated the market and was a preserve of a few. So they exchanged 'missiles', as letters were nicknamed. One memorable 'missile' he wrote to her rang in his mind. He let her know that he loved her deeply. Stella was good in English. So he did not want to let himself down.

> *Dearest Stella,*
>
> *I am studying hard to make butter and bread as our teachers said when they punished the noise, and not us. However your beauty has ever left my heart drumming in my rib cage, my classmate. It has made me spend sleepless nights staring up blankly dreaming about us together some day. It has made me conceive the idea that one sweet day we shall walk down the aisle just like our teachers, Dorothy and Mark.*
>
> *My love for you is stronger than steel, as jealous as two cockerel in a homestead fighting for survival. It burns*

inside like the blazing plane on a crash, in summer. Nothing stands to substitute it for when it rains, the waters flow and leave it untouched; and when it dries, it stands stronger and healthier, non-withered like the lily by the waterside. I'll borrow any book to protect it. Make your dreams come true by studying harder.

FM

Musa folded the letter nicely and inserted it in a small white envelope and posted it at Maseno post office during one of the school outings.

During their secondary school they only met once in a cultural festival at Kisumu. Musa's encounter with Stella in college was accidental. One afternoon, he had paid a visit to Judy in her hostel. He strolled from his hostel and knocked on Judy's door. It was opened by Stella. Judy was not in. They stared at each other in disbelief and with quizzical expressions. Well, Musa was not sure whether he was seeing well or dreaming. Much time had elapsed since they last met at the Kisumu cultural festival. Stella radiated her adorned childhood charms which were now enhanced in her maturity. She was now a young beautiful woman.

"So long! Stella? What are you doing here? You're the last person I expected here! Is it you?" Several questions came to his mind.

"It is me Fred. You can't believe it, I know," Stella answered gently in an equivocal voice. "The world is small, people meet, and it is mountains that don't."

They hugged. Stella was no longer the shy little girl he had known in school. Time had changed her greatly.

"It is me Fred." She rested her head on Musa's shoulder as he stroked her back gently. It was like a reunion of long lost siblings who had returned home when everyone had long forgotten about them. They disengaged and stared at each other. Stella's eyes were beautiful and intelligent.

"How have you been?" Stella inquired.

"I've been doing well," Musa answered.

"It has been a long time since we last saw each other in Kisumu. Honestly, I never ever expected to meet you. Time has changed you. Now you are an old man with a bush on your face. I am hardly able to recognize you," Stella joked amidst laughter. "Had we met in the streets, I would have passed right by you without a second thought. I'm really happy to see you again." She held Musa's hand and led him to the room.

Stella sat on the bed while Musa took an adjacent seat. The cubicle was small.

"I'm a visitor here. I came to see Judy. We have been good friends since our days in secondary school. She was my dorm mate and classmate at Lugulu and on top, a great friend. Since then our ties have been close. We do the same course, though I'm in K.U campus," she explained. Stella was a second year B.A student at Kenyatta University.

Stella had had a desire to meet Musa, but hills and valleys had stood between them. The memories marked a reawakening of her feelings towards Musa which she found difficult to hide, but she already knew that Judy had already taken the helm.

"Judy is you fiancée?" She propped sarcastically.

Musa had looked down trying to evade the question. He had to be tactical to answer her question without hurting her. Women can be jealous if their rights are violated, and Stella was no exception.

"What's your guess?"

"I am not an angel, but I can guess," she answered.

Musa lied, "we're good friends."

"I know you just lied," she objected.

"How do you know?"

"I am a magician," Stella laughed. "Judy tells me about a Musa, but it never crossed my mind that she is talking about the Musa of Manga, my former classmate." One could detect the envy in her words. "I wish you all the best," she concluded.

They revisited their past, their times at Manga and their days in primary school. Her father was a teacher in the neighbouring school, but was now retired and settled in Kisumu.

Throughout college he met Stella several times. Again they became close acquaintances having shared a past. Stella was sure Musa and Judy were cemented together and nothing could separate them, but deep within her heart, she envied Judy and harboured feelings for Musa which she discretely and freely expressed in their rapport while together in the absence of Judy.

Chapter Eleven

It was approaching five o'clock in the evening and Uhuru Park was getting more crowded. People were breaking from their offices to head home. Musa stood and cleaned some stubborn grass from the back of his shirt and pair of trousers and then walked slowly to Stella's office. Stella had been lucky. Using her connections, she had landed a job at the ministry of transport as a purchasing officer. He wanted to meet her before she left the office. He loved her and wanted to assure her that without a job or a source of income, he was confident to tell her as much. Roles were changing from the traditional ones where men were breadwinners and women were recipients, courtesy of modern education and a spirited campaign in female empowerment, which had made in-roads to the legislation. With more and more women being financially empowered, women too were becoming breadwinners. Really, love does not see material things, he thought, and if it sees, then it is a fake one that cannot stand the test of time.

Stella was walking down the staircase with a group of work mates, chatting. She was in a jovial mood dressed smartly in a navy blue suit, white blouse and darting fashionable high heeled opened toed shoes.

"Tell me where you're going," she gently tapped Musa's shoulder from the side.

"To your office," he answered jovially as he turned his head. "You look neat in this attire. How much did you cough up for it? It must have been imported from mars."

"It cost the world. All my first pay went in to my repair," she joked.

Her smiles were alluring, her hand radiated warmth

and her body emitted a powerful hibiscus scent.

"It feels good to see you. Seeing you alone fills my stomach." Musa was passionate. They walked slowly, chatting towards the city centre.

"Can we take tea?" Stella suggested.

"I would love to. Sure," he replied. Musa hadn't taken a meal that day. He had nothing in his pockets.

Within a few minutes, they were seated in the park cafe enjoying the evening and taking tea with snacks. For Musa, it was a meal he couldn't afford and in a way it was his supper. But Stella was to foot the bill as she always did. They drank, ate, joked and laughed. Well, an evening like this was what Musa yearned for to temporarily forget the harsh reality of life.

Then Musa held Stella's palm, squeezed it gently and let it loose. He stroked her cheeks softly, left and right. It gave her a delightful sensation. She appreciated it with a shy smile, and her dimples played cheerfully. In every way, she resembled her mother, whose generosity was a legend in Manga. Musa remembered the saying, "*nyang'era rotung'i na mori yaye rotung'i. Etakogwa eng'ina n'ekogwa ise.* Meaning nyangera, a horned cow, has the characteristics of the parents and if it does not resemble the mother it takes the characteristics of the father." Stella resembled her mother in every way. Her generosity, her umber radiance, her soft smooth tone, her unassuming smile and mannerisms were epitomized in her mother.

"I'm grateful for the meal. I've not had a meal today," Musa sincerely thanked Stella. "Meals are out of reach for job seekers."

"It is me that should be thanking you for accepting my treat. It is just a simple treat. Remember, I was on the streets for a long time with you," she informed. "On a good day, a plain potato chip made my day."

Musa looked at Stella's eyes. They were sharp intelligent eyes. He appreciated her gesture. He was under pressure from his home to marry. He was feeling old enough to have a family. He did not know how long it would take to have a job. With or without a job, he needed to have a family. He resolved. And Stella was the chosen one. "I've something for you tonight my dear," Musa chose his words carefully to convey the message. "Something greater than you can imagine." He emphasized. "And kindly promise that you won't let me down."

"I need to hear it first then give my opinion," Stella answered.

"Stella, I've not told you. You're so good, so kind and considerate. You buy me a meal when I cannot return the favour, and you entertain me when I am jobless. You're the love of my life. Kindly accept my love and my hand in marriage," he proposed.

There was total silence between the two except for the soft piped blues percolating into the room from the red carpeted walls.

> *Love love*
> *Is great at the right time*
> *Love love*
> *Is a mysterious wind blowing in the desert*
> *And no one can stop it*
> *Love love*
> *Are strong waves in the ocean*
> *Love love*
> *Is a fierce fire in the wilderness*

Love was ok. She felt it and needed it. But marriage was a thorn in the flesh for Stella. "I don't know really what to say. I'm elated that my worth as a woman has been recognized. But you cannot climb a tree from the top. I've always told you that," she posed and stared at Musa. "While the idea is good, your immediate goal is to get a job. This does not mean I'm not interested. I am. But it would be hard to raise a family without an income. Life would be rough for both of us," Stella explained politely and empathetically.

Musa surveyed the ceiling. It was polished mahogany to reflect the floor. Stella was right. Perhaps he had raised his proposal at an inappropriate time or she wanted not to appear cheap. This was the third time she had refused his hand in marriages sighting several reasons. True, times had changed with traditional families taking a back stage. Traditional roles within the family had been revised unconsciously with women bringing even more to the family table than men. Even though this was a reality, a man who brings nothing to the home, the marriage may end up strained. His ego may be punctured, ending up with an inferiority complex and eventually a dysfunctional family.

"You may be right Stella. God willing, the doors may be opened soon. I've done all it takes. I am now ready to try _jua kali_ as an alternative. What I lack is finances," he sounded distant. "May be soon, God will hear my prayers." He surveyed the ceiling again with his hands supporting his chin.

"I have known you all along," she replied. "You're one man I really admire, your perseverance notwithstanding, your positive attitude to life, and your acceptance to the changing times. Your determination, and sincere approach to issues and of course your love," Stella smiled. "I love you, but you must realize our cultural differences are there. You are a Gusii and I'm a Luo. Will that blend be acceptable across the divide? Yes, I love you and I can say I do very much. Will love alone be enough to take us through? Won't your people feel that you have gone beyond their norms and wonder whether there are no better girls from your home to marry?" Her face was imploring, bright and confident. "Further, I've several obligations for myself and my family. First, I need to settle down and enjoy the sweat of my education at least for a year before the little ones come so that I can find time for them, and I need to assist my siblings with school fees. Will that auger well in a family set up? I must uplift the burden of my parents by seeing my brothers through school. It is one way I can appreciate the struggle, sacrifice, and support they put in bringing me up without a scar and educating me."

Stella had a lovely melodious voice with a little tinge of Luo accent. Musa admired her as she spoke. He needed her most to tell him "sorry" for the way the world was treating him. He stretched his hand to have a feel with his index finger of the soft fabric she wore. It defined her bottle figure. Her limbs were fleshy. Stella was an amazing woman and a good person to spend time with. He was suddenly reminded of Judy, his first love, and he couldn't fail to note a world of difference. Stella was kind, appreciative, and sincere, while Judy was elusive, mysterious and unreliable.

Musa was lost for words. He did not know how best to win Stella, but he was determined. Like a lion whose life depended on its prey, he repeated, "I love you with a job or without one. I need your presence every moment in my life. I'll do all I can to fulfill your wishes, and if you say a later date, I'll take it and do as you wish. I have absolutely no power over your decisions, the way you have no power over my love for you," he pleaded.

Stella was divided. She felt uneasy. There was a moment of silence when the soft blues continued to percolate through the room with sweet lyrics and captivating tunes. She felt hollow and incomplete. She was approaching twenty six and she was under intense pressure from her own mother to have her own house. Yes, she loved Musa very much. Her love for him stemmed back from days in primary. She knew, somehow, that he could be trusted to take the helm. All along, there had been barriers and hurdles to conquer. Yet, after all the barriers and hurdles had been surmounted, maybe all of them, her desire to advance her career and meet her family's obligations while still single glared and stood in her way. Then Musa's joblessness reared its tentacles. She felt confused and unable to decide. She let her head rest on her right palm. In his moment of quietness, Stella was distant.

Her father, Onyango, was a teacher in Manga. Soon after her K.C.P.E, he was transferred to Kisumu, their ancestral home. The family had to move with him. She never saw Musa again except for the cultural week in Kisumu. And when they met in college, Judy, though unwittingly, stood between them. And now, Musa's joblessness stood unpleasantly between them. It was like a chain reaction that was destined to go on and on without ever coming to an end. She felt, she needed to reexamine her priorities and put them right.

"Suppose, just suppose, your people don't like the idea of us getting married?" she asked.

"Why do you think they would object?" he inquired.

"You and I don't come from the same ethnic background. I'm a Luo and uncircumcised," she pressed on. "And Manga had a lot of respect for its culture. I guess much has not changed."

"That was Manga then. Cultural conflicts shouldn't stand between us. These are modern times now. We are the change agents. Today, who advocates circumcision of girls? The church and the government have convinced the community against the dangers of girl circumcision. Even in Manga, circumcision of girls is now not a norm. Further you're not marrying the community. It's me, Fredrick Musa. The nucleus family now has more say than the extended family in matters of family life. Times have changed greatly, bringing in new ideas into our once stubborn cultures courtesy of modern education and religion. They have done disservice to our old culture, tearing them apart and integrating them into new ways of thinking and doing things," Musa explained. "Stella, can you imagine that my father is now baptized with a Christian name, Paul. He is no longer shouting and fighting imaginary enemies or *earare*, the pepper he was when drunk."

"You mean?" Stella was a gap with surprise.

"He prays every morning and evening asking God, not *engoro,* or his ancestors to take charge and care of his burdens," he laughed gently. "And the last time I was at home, he said, 'son, I know you have interacted outside our community. Do not tie yourself down so much. All people are God's people.' It is only my uncle, Nyakundi who still clenches onto traditions. But time and Christianity are softening his stand."

"Suppose, just suppose Judy reappeared?" Stella did not want to leave anything to chance, "how will you handle two women?"

"Judy lost when you won," he replied. "She could never win now, even if she used magic charms."

Stella leaned slightly on Musa's chest. He let her fall on it. She looked at him with bright eyes. It was a romantic evening with a surrounding to match the occasion. Darkness had fallen in, but through the widow, the moon and the street lights illuminated the streets. She stretched her hand and touched a potted rose flower on the table. She briefly admired it. Then, she turned and looked at Musa in the eyes with her weak defeated eyes, almost sleepy. "Musa my darling, can I trust you to navigate the ship?" She implored.

"Yes you can," he replied calmly. "I'll navigate it to the end, through the stormy sea of life."

"I love you," she responded weakly on his arms.

"Will you marry me?" Musa posed again, this time in a whisper.

"Yes," Stella replied weakly, almost to herself.

"When?" He asked her excitedly.

"Any time you want. Any time you want." She repeated

That evening Musa had jumped over a very high hurdle in life and maybe that was the reason he slept more soundly than ever before.

Chapter Twelve

Inside the sprawling and expansive Maasai Mara National Park, a lioness roared lazily in the afternoon heat. She was not bothered with the many tourists' vehicles and the cameras flicking and clicking on and off on her way. Her echoes resonated several miles away. Her three cubs woke up from the afternoon nap jostling and wrestling one another. Another pride of lions responded in accord from the other ridge. In unison, the plain echoed to their roars. The gazelles grazing nearby took off at high speeds all in one direction. Gazelles and lions have never been friends. There is a myth tale that a lion and a gazelle were good friends. The lion left its cub with the gazelle, but accidentally the gazelle trampled on it. The lion never forgave the gazelle and hunted it for food. Therefore, instinct told the gazelles that there was looming danger of an attack. A herd of elephants a short distance away continued to forage on the vegetation undisturbed. Perhaps, because of their size and immense strength, to them nothing much mattered. Not a threat from other animals.

The birds of the park flew from one tree to another. They seemingly sang freedom songs, political tunes, religious melodies and other familiar cultural rhythms. They seemed happy and thankful to their creator for the daily bread that they hardly worked for. Others danced their heads and tails in response to these songs. Even the grazing animals scattered in the plains seemed to respond to the music with the occasional wag of their tails or just a nod. They were in a festive mood.

It was a beautiful clear day with the sun shining high in the sky and its rays piercing ruthlessly through the space. Judy watched the animals, some racing and others grazing in merriment. She had only seen lions and gazelles on television and in cinema. Now she was watching them in real life and she enjoyed every bit of it. These sceneries accorded several tourists rare opportunities to watch; and to film these scenes and enjoy themselves.

Beside the open Toyota Land Cruiser, Richard Morgans lay on his back supporting his head on a high density pillow which was an extension of a cream portable mattress. He slept peacefully oblivious of what was going on around him. He was tall man, slightly bulky with hairy and athletic legs. He wore a white short sleeved T-shirt, a matching pair of shorts and a pair of cream safari boots. A small white tent was pitched beside him, partially protecting him from the scorching tropical sun.

Judy looked at him with a slight youthful smile on her face. Her looks were enhanced with a naughty smile playing on her chocolate lips. She moved and sat on the cream mattress closer to Richard. Inside, she felt a glowing desire to kiss him. She tapped his cheek lightly and bent over, giving him a slight kiss on his left cheek. She knew the battle was won and as his special girl, she wanted it to be that way. She felt lucky to have a man of his calibre: someone with money, handsome and generous at showering her with classic romance she had only seen in movies. Most importantly, he had the money. God knows, she needed the money. Badly.

Richard's love for coastal beaches and swimming in the coastal waters was immense. This in part explained why he was a frequent visitor to Kenya. To him, money was not the problem. He had a lot of it. His parents back in the U.K. were well-to-do and owned manufacturing and supply chain businesses. And being the only child in the family, all the wealth was at his disposal to make him happy. In addition, Kenya was one of the established market outlets for his businesses.

Whenever he visited Kenya, Richard usually came with boxes full of drugs which Judy assisted to distribute to his already established market outlets within the city. It is a market that had grown over time. Calvin and Fatima also assisted in the distribution. He paid them well. This improved their financial status substantially. They were doing well financially. The business fetched good money and in return, Richard appreciated Judy's efforts by paying her handsomely in salary, tips and allowances.

With this money, Judy had bought herself a new salon car, a limousine, and settled in her own posh house in an upmarket area of the city, away from her uncle's family who had kept a watchful eye on her. She was also able to meet her daily requirements comfortably with little struggle. Now, she no longer dreamed of getting another job. No. It was not important. She already had more than a job. What preoccupied her mind was how to please Richard who now meant the world to her. He was a wonderful lover who had literally squeezed out her innocence and opened her eyes to a world she had not known: the world of romance and money. It was like discovering hidden treasure at the right time.

With a pious mother, Judy had learnt from the early age that beer was bad and only ladies of loose morals took it. Richard had slowly introduced her to it and now she could drain bottle after bottle without fear of getting drunk, as if she had been drinking all her life.

It was now more than two years since she had left the university with a BA degree. She was only twenty-four and in the prime of her life. Soon she would be turning twenty-five, but she still felt young. When she joined the job market, she had a glowing desire to get a well-paying job, a dream of any graduate. Even with the hard economic times, and the emerged culture of patronage, kickbacks and nepotism in the job market, Judy had not anticipated a problem in securing a job. To her it was a small and exciting game that was to last a few days. She banked her hope on her father who was once in the influential circles. But time had proved her wrong. It had proved very difficult to get one. The government had frozen hiring for all public service jobs under the pretext that there were no funds to meet recurrent expenditures. Friendly countries had frozen any form of aid sighting corruption and mismanagement of funds. The World Bank and the International Monetary Fund were hard on the government. Days had passed into months and then two years down the line, Richard appeared as her saviour.

Her father's home consumer goods company had not done well. There was excessive competition from well established firms with more sound capital base, giving them greater aggressiveness and comparative advantage. The banks' interest rates on borrowed capital were too high. Coupled with the diminishing purchasing power of the populace he opted to settle back in his rural home to try farming on his ten acre piece of land after retiring from the civil service.

The farming business was not lucrative either with the liberalized market economy. Inputs were expensive but the prices of the products were always low. The roads were impassable especially during the rainy seasons. This made it hard to reach the markets where prices were favourable. Even when the roads were passable, the produces reached the market when their quality had deteriorated. Coupled with the unpredictable weather patterns, the risks and uncertainties were always too high. The profit margins were further compromised.

With the low income, it meant that life had to be adjusted downwards. This did not augur well to the children, especially Judy who had been brought up exclusively in the city and always received all the softer things in life. It meant more struggle, and forgoing some things they termed essential.

The sun burned with more intense heat every moment. The sky was clear with only a few very distant white clouds in sight. It had not rained for some time now and there were no signs of it. The country-side was so dry that some rivers had dried up. The park vegetation of the predominant acacia and the strong-willed elephant grass were turning brownish. However, some stubborn patches demonstrated their shrewd nature to withstand such adversity using their innate adaptive nature. Their determination to live on and on despite the odds were yielding some dividends. If human beings could be like this grass, they would survive in any situations, she reasoned. She was strong-willed like the elephant grass.

Judy looked toward the direction where they had come from; far beyond the plains and over the smoky hills to the north. Nairobi was in that direction. She felt calm being in the country side far from the city. She knew Nairobi well, having been brought up there.

Her mind flushed back to college. She remembered Musa, the young man she had met there and declared to him her virgin love. He was handsome and kind, qualities any girl could envy. But he had been overtaken by events. She had already made up her mind once and for all. Musa was not her man. He was not her size to begin with, nor did he represent her emerging aspirations. He was several castes below her. He was an ass without a cent; and without money love could not be sustained. It could not thrive to grant joy and everlasting happiness. Musa had his own problems. She had her own problems to solve too. He needed money to spring himself up from his poor status to a reasonably noble one, and this was remote. Only then could their love have a guarantee of everlasting joy. With her powers as a woman, she had learnt and become a master of manipulation.

With the new revelations, Judy needed money and all the happiness that money could offer. It gave her a new sense of being and hopes for her dreams: a modern house, a model car and many good things money could afford. She felt that she owed Fatima a great deal for being instrumental in opening her eyes of ignorance and ushering in a new revelation that opened a new chapter.

Her craving for money and what she termed "the good life" was enhanced further. She reasoned that, had Richard Morgans not had money, he could not have come to Kenya. They could not have met or even gone to Masaai Mara where they had spent fortunes in a span of two days. She looked at her Rolex watch. It was approaching four o'clock. She tapped Richard's shoulder softly, "Richie." She called him, "Richie, wake up now. It is time to go."

Richard stretched his hands sideways without opening his eyes, but with a feeble smile unconsciously playing on his lips. He inhaled deeply and let it flow out freely. He reached out at Judy's neck and pulled her to himself. She let him have his way. Then he gave her a long hearty kiss in embrace.

"Isn't it sweet that way?" Judy inquired shyly. She felt she was now the special girl Richard dreamt about and she wasn't going to let him think of any other woman. No, she wasn't. She had a resolute mind. She was there for him and she was happy that way. In this mood she silently thanked God for having been born that beautiful. Her heart beat hard, harder in anticipation. She swallowed a bunch of warm saliva as they stared at each other eye to eye. They were bright, warm and imploring eyes with sheets of tears.

"I'll cheat to say it isn't," Richard said it plainly. "It is sweeter than honey."

"Me too. You're a wonderful golden boy," she flattered him.

"You mean?" He laughed a little confidently and a little nervously. "It is nice to hear that."

"It is good to hear that again from your own mouth," she said.

"Now, time is not our side. We only have this afternoon here left. Tomorrow we need to go back to Nairobi in time and make arrangements for our travel to London. We still have a few boxes of drugs to deliver to our customers. We need to act fast before time catches up with us. Good business is about keeping time and not disappointing customers," Richard explained.

Judy was looking forward to the day she would fly in an airplane. This reminder added more excitement in her heart. In one week's time she was flying aboard a British Airway flight to London with her fiancé Richard. Her heart raced in her rib cage. "Richie, I have to go home and inform my parents about our flight to London. They'll be delighted to hear the good news, and then I shall come back in time for the journey."

"It's alright, that way," he held her arm as they entered their vehicle.

"Certainly," she affirmed.

Then Richard drove off slowly towards the park lodge admiring the Fauna and Flora of the sprawling Maasai Mara National Park, and the enchanting landscape with big umbrella trees, with sleepy small but distinct rolling hills, and few small valleys at their borders.

Chapter Thirteen

When luck knocks, no one has powers to hold it back. It may delay giving feelings of disillusionment, but luck has its powers, and cannot be prevailed upon. Finally, Musa's tribulations turned to fortunes. He sat in his office smiling to himself remembering back then. He had come a long way. He had been in this office for only six months. He was happy that at last his prayers had been answered. Though not handsomely paying to cater for his many needs, he had landed a job after several years of frustration in the city as a job seeker. The pains and struggles were still in his mind, though he was trying hard to put the past behind him and forge forward.

It was a Friday, and the culture he found in the office was that Fridays were lazy days. Many workmates did not stay long in the office. Some made technical appearances, hanged their coats on the chairs and disappeared. Having experienced the hardship of landing a job, he was determined to impress and earn justly. He usually worked for long hours compared to some senior employees in his department. This had already earned him a name in his department as a workaholic. He was efficient and thorough. He worked on his last file and placed it in the tray labelled 'out'. Then he stood up from his chair, stretched out and walked across the room to the open window. A fresh breeze of air hit his face. He looked outside as far as his eyes could see, then to the city centre where he spent years as a job seeker. Life had become a long dramatic journey, but determination to continue and encouragement from well-wishers kept him going amidst the hardship and had yielded dividends at last.

It was one o'clock. Musa left his office and took a lift to the ground floor. From there he walked slowly past the Uchumi Supermarket to the Ambassador Restaurant for lunch. He crossed the Moi Avenue and then made his way through a car park. Just as he was about to enter the restaurant someone tapped him on his shoulder. He turned his head to see who it was. He froze. It was unmistakably Judy Nyanchera Makosa, his college mate. It was really unexpected to see Judy. He stared at her. Their eyes met again in the air and held there for a long time. She was glamorous. It was three years since he saw her last. During those graceful seconds, Musa noticed that Judy had changed greatly from a simple urban lady to a strikingly mature woman with an air of importance all around her.

He had tried to locate her in the city and in her rural home without success. Mobile technology had not caught up by then, so he wrote her letters and sweet poems reminding her of their wonderful times together and their promises. He invoked in them their best memories together. Judy was enthusiastic at the beginning, but then she asked not to be disturbed. What could one expect of a young man in love with a woman whose love was mysterious? His ego was hurt. He felt cheated by a woman he had placed a lot of his hope in. To add insult to injury, his joblessness troubled him. He could not understand the once enthusiastic Judy. "Could it be that she had met someone else?" He always wondered. Well, in a few minutes he was sure that he was going to have answers to all his questions." Unknown to him, life in the city as a job seeker had taught Judy lessons. In the process, she had rediscovered herself, developed new and parallel interests, expectations and character. She had no room for him anymore. She did not uphold marriage. These two were heaped on the financially successful men and women. Musa's love was insignificant without money to sustain it. She knew that she was beautiful and she could use this power and charm to draw in any man around her with money. In a short stint, she had Richard Morgans, the English businessman who showered her with money and classic romance. She could get bank managers, politicians, businessmen, lawyers and many men with money and influence.

"Musa!" Judy shouted at him in disbelief. "Are you the one I'm seeing or am I dreaming?" She wasn't quite sure whether it was him.

Musa's heart bounded with a mixture of excitement and anxiety. "What a pleasant surprise." He stretched his hand out to greet her. He gave her a heart-warming smile as she fell on his shoulder. He tapped her back gently as they hugged each other. What next could two lost friends do? People passing by watched them as the graceful moments tickled on. When they disengaged, their armpits were dripping with sweat, their eyes silvery and their entire bodies shaking from a rekindled flame. They stared at each other again. Musa was the embodiment of the dreams of yester years. He was handsome, tall and with sharp intelligent eyes. In that matching black double-breasted suit with a white shirt, a black tie and black shoes, he looked like an executive of some prestigious organization. Judy was calm with a distant look. She had not expected to see him. She drew in a heavy gulp of air and let it flow out freely through her nostrils.

"Musa, I'm excited to see you after such a long time," Judy recovered first. "Where have you been hiding all a long? You have changed from that small little boy I knew to a charming man," she equipped the joke with a shy captivating laughter.

Musa stared at her with calm and composed eyes. He wasn't sure whether it was real or a dream he was undergoing. A transitional silence followed. When their eyes met again, Judy felt her heart melting in a pot of love.

Musa took his courage and spoke calmly, "You've been lost Judy," he said, "so lost. I tried to trace you everywhere I could think of finding you, but in vain. I went to your home and inquired of your whereabouts. Your mum told me that you had come to the city. Using the new address she gave me, I tried to contact you several times. I didn't get any reply. Had you gone to mars?"

"I don't know what really happened. We just lost one another," She lied defensively.

"Separation of two friends is a painful experience and the worry of your whereabouts broke my heart," he posed with a smile.

He was now recovering well from the initial shock of meeting Judy unexpectedly. His adrenaline level was going down. "It is great to see you after so long."

Judy held Musa's hand and led him into the restaurant. "We can talk while we eat," she said. "I can't deny it," she said to herself, "an old flame hasn't extinguished yet. It umbers and simmers quietly. But the beautiful things I desire in life, perhaps he can't afford or he will never be able too. Yes, he was the guy who first taught me how to dance during my hey days in college, and through whom the moonlight shone. We often danced together to the soft heartwarming blues which left our hearts melting. Somehow, after all the fun I've had, I need to settle down with the one man I love. Maybe."

They took seats opposite each other at an empty table. "This restaurant cooks tasty chicken. I think I'll have the chicken and chips," she took the menu and studied it.

"I wouldn't mind the same. Remember, I always loved chicken in college," Musa remarked jokingly.

When the waiter came to serve them, Judy ordered for two plates of grilled chicken served with chips and cold mango juice.

As the waiter left to prepare their orders, Musa felt that his questions deserved some answers, "to begin with, where did you disappear to without a trace?" he propped.

Judy looked down and wanted to evade the question. "I have been in Nairobi. It is a tough exercise to be in Nairobi, but I tackled it."

"I built you a very special palace in my heart and laid down a red carpet on which you walked on day and night," Musa said rhetorically.

"And what happened?" she inquired with startled eyes.

"You refused to walk on it?" he brazenly joked, "and went to oblivion."

"I'm here now."

They ate their lunch slowly as they shared experiences. They talked a lot to cover for the lost time. There was a certain dignity on how Judy handled issues with more experience than before.

"Do people have to go through so much pain in the name of love?" Musa asked.

Judy placed her spoon on her plate and held Musa's left finger: The engagement index. "I love you Musa. I want to ask you one question." She squeezed the fingers harder.

"I'll answer," he replied as he stared at her eyes.

"Do you still love me? Is the red carpet you placed for me still there?"

"Judy," he started without looking at her. "When a fast flowing river encounters a barrier that it cannot go through, what does it do?"

Judy did not reply immediately. She kept quiet for a while then said, "nothing," then she pondered and said, "it just doesn't stop and calls it a day. It flows on."

"Yes. It doesn't stop and call it a day. It flows on," he repeated. "It breaks the barrier or changes its course."

"So you have found a woman and changed course?" Judy's eyes shone a silver sheet of tears. However, she managed to put on a feeble, but inviting smile. "Musa, from today I am all yours till the bright sun ceases to shine."

Her tone had a lot of seriousness. This made Musa feel hollow deep inside. The emptiness was multiplied further by the fact that Judy's love had seemed rather mysterious, hidden and now coming at a time it was likely to divide him into two. He had initially laid his heart bare for her, all his love, yet she did not keep her promises. He wondered whether she would keep them this time around.

In this state of confusion, Musa toyed with the idea of having two girlfriends. It was an emerging trend of city life. The opportunity had presented two girls from who to choose from a partner in marriage, Stella the childhood love and now Judy, the beautiful urban pageant. But it was a paradox. The same night he was going to be travelling to his rural home, Manga, with Stella to introduce her to his parents and the village as his wife-to-be. The outcome perhaps could determine Judy's fate. If his parents and the village refused to bless their marriage due to cultural reasons, he would have to press on and convince them that Stella was not a Luo but a woman meant for him. If Stella's parents became an obstacle in the way, she was to persuade them to yield. If there was no chance of ever convincing them, he had to respect the elders' opinion and their culture. Then Judy stood some chance of winning. This remained his secret, and he did not want to reveal it to Judy.

"What have you been doing since?" Musa wanted to know more

"I do business. I import second hand clothes and I also work with a pharmaceutical company with its headquarters in London.

Judy had grown to talk big and lie without detection. She was a manipulator, an opportunist and was using a number of men in a number of ways to achieve what she wanted. The same men were also using her to achieve what they wanted. Only in some cases, she was too naïve to realize it.

"That is great for you," Musa remarked, "then you must be really enterprising. In a way I envy your good successes," he encouraged her.

"Maybe, but I am just trying to survive in the city as a job seeker, one needs to think outside the box. Tomorrow, I shall be travelling to London on a business trip. I've already formalized my travel arrangements," she informed him.

"Really?" he equipped. "To London? You've made a leap on your life. I envy you."

She answered with a confident tone, "I look forward to seeing you when I'm back in a month."

She opened her black leather bag, removed a thousand shillings and a business card. She handed the card to Musa, "this is my phone number to my house. Please call me in a month and we shall arrange to meet again and have all the fun in the world."

He took the card and looked at it. She was the marketing executive of R.M pharmaceutical company (k) ltd. Meanwhile Judy paid the waiters for the two lunches.

"I stay at Runda next to the shopping centre," she informed, "I'm more than glad to meet you, but I must leave now to tend to other issues." She stood up from her chair and led the way out. Musa followed her to a car park outside the hotel where Judy had parked her black limousine. She stopped beside it and opened the driver's door. Soft blues music played from the background, "it is too late to love me now."

"This is my car. How do you like it?" She asked jovially.

"It's a nice one," he commented. The car was real executive with navy blue velvet seats and sparkling clean.

"This is my second car. I sold my first car, a Toyota Corolla, a few days ago," she informed him.

It was clear that Judy had laid her hands on good money. The fact that she lived in a posh estate, and drove an exclusively high class car attested to that. Her father had been a senior civil servant and successful businessman. This could have been part of her inheritance. He could not compare himself to her. While he started from scratch, Judy must have had a kick start from somewhere.

She placed her hand on his shoulder. "I have to meet my business associate at two o'clock." It was a few minutes to two now. She drew in a punch of air as she gave Musa the last farewell hug with a promise to meet again. "See you when I'm back," she said. She entered her vehicle and rattled the engine. Musa waved at her as she drove off amidst the jam. He stood rooted at the car park for some time. The two had gone to school together, done the same courses and he always excelled more than her, but destiny had really been a paradox. She was driving a sleek car, and he was not even dreaming of owning a junk one soon. "One's destiny is shaped by many unforeseen forces and some of them remain too strong to control," he observed silently.

He watched the vehicle roll away until she made her last bend. Before she disappeared she waved back again. Musa waved to her in return. Then he made his last silent observations, "many loves aren't sustained by the youths who are still learning and meeting the current challenges. As youthful years pass by, attitudes may change too, bringing about a new state of perception. Other than the fact that she had possessed my heart, I had wanted her to occupy my mind forever, but now there is Stella too," he posed.

Chapter Fourteen

It was approaching five o'clock. Musa sat on his red velvet swivel chair staring at the roof. He swung gently from left to right. The office telephone on the right side of the table rang twice. It had been replaced recently. He held the head receiver and put it closer to his ear. He was expecting Stella's call. He shouted hello several times, but the phone went unanswered. He replaced the receiver on its stand and looked at his watch, a present front Stella for an arbitrary birthday fixed for convenience. Musa's parents had not had a chance to attend school. They did not know how to read and write, so they never kept records of births of their children. Somehow, he knew that he was born at a time when mysterious wind was the cause of a torrential rain that filled the streams, swept crops down steam and aftermath cholera that left every one holding onto a tree. The rains uprooted trees and left the land bare in many parts of the country. The ranges of Manga were left gapping in gullies. He was named when a white missionary came to the village and erected a church to give hope to the village and convert souls to Christ.

All his sisters and brothers were born at home with the assistance of traditional midwives. The only hospital around was kilometres away. With extremely poor means of communication, vehicle transportation was rare as roads were often rendered impassable during the rainy seasons. Roads were always mucky, pot-holed and slippery. The few which defied the odds to operate were miserably frustrated by numerous breakdowns on the way. Somehow, it was uneconomical to operate a *matatu* on these roads as vehicles were only taken in cases of emergency.

At around quarter to five, there was a soft knock on the door. Musa jumped in excitement. He adjusted his coat and tie in readiness to meet the visitor. The door flung open and his secretary walked in carrying a pile of files. She was bringing in more work for the next week. He had expected Stella to walk in. He greeted the secretary unconcerned and motioned her to place the files on the empty space on the table. He stood from his chair and walked across the window whistling softly. "*Obosisa mbwari Kiko ee. Onyare atabwati twoni, anga bosisa mbwaita,* scabies attacked Kiko. Had he not had a cock, the scabies could have killed him." She placed the files gently on the table and as if not to disturb him, walked out quickly closing the door behind her.

Stella was an elegant, black, tall woman. She had big eyes floating in her sockets. But they made her appear ever alert and intelligent. Her subtle charms, humour and developed mannerisms were inviting. After that long separation and their subsequent re-encounter in college, Stella had grown up to a beautiful young woman. She was less talkative as compared to Judy. Her encouraging smile always motivated him to soldier on in the midst of adversity. Her jokes were humorous and always intelligent. Given her simple upbringing in the village, she loved a simple and inexpensive lifestyle, and she was always choosing her friends wisely.

When Stella's father was transferred from Musa's rural primary school, Manga to Kisumu, the family moved to live with him in the same school he was to teach. She could not understand what was happening then. She was too young to understand. With the mountainous landscape and the many small rivers cutting them right at the valleys, books became her constant companion. She loved reading and she read harder every day. Her teachers and parents encouraged her. She preferred groups of girls in her class who also excelled in their academic work. With the passage of time, memories of Musa were fading and she only thought of passing her examinations and becoming an important person in society. She developed the ambition of breaking the monotony of the village life where women laboured all day long cultivating the obstinate pieces of land, fetching water, firewood, and performing never-ending manual duties.

She detested the outright poverty, low level of literacy and ignorance that was widespread in the village. Her tour to Kisumu and Nairobi international trade fair shows as a student had increased her desire to live in town when she grew up and became independent. She hoped to get a job in Nairobi where she could meet Musa or any other man who she could sincerely fall in love with, marry and have a family of her own. These ambitions helped her excel through primary school as well as secondary school to join the prestigious Kenyatta University.

There was commotion in the corridors. Musa pulled up his left shirt sleeve. Again, it exposed his memorable digital watch. It read 5:30 p.m. He looked at the streets. They were becoming crowded with people and vehicles. *Matatus* and buses were hooting, luring passengers to board them. People were breaking for their weekend. It was Friday and Stella was to come over in time for their long journey to the village of Manga. What could have happened? She never failed him at any moment and she was always very punctual.

Almost immediately, there was a soft, almost distinct, knock at the door. Musa walked to the door and turned the handle. The door flung open and Stella strode in broadly smiling radiating her subtle charms. She was elegantly dressed for the big occasion. They looked each other in the eyes for a second. In their eyes there were unmistakable messages written which the duo understood too well. They were meant for each other. They were made to plan their future together and fly in the same direction.

That night they travelled to the village of Manga. Musa was going to formally introduce Stella as his wife-to-be to his parents and to the entire village.

Chapter Fifteen

Musa conceded that he loved Stella. There were qualities about her that made her more special than Judy. Yes, both of them were glamorously beautiful. But Stella was bewitching while Judy was mysteriously subtle. Even when Judy had a real edge over Stella and they had met at the right time: She had cultural and ethnic advantage given the reality at the village of Manga that felt he should marry a girl who understood their customs; Judy had disappointed him when he needed her most. She had been mysterious, indifferent and elusive. She had disappeared from him when he needed her most to tell him "sorry" when the times were hard pressing. Judy had only reappeared mysteriously as she had disappeared to confuse him further. He was convinced, that Judy had only remembered rather too late that her luck lay on Musa after perpetual failure in her romantic exploits elsewhere.

Stella had a special past in his history and heart. He had seen her grow up as a young girl and had imparted in his heart a virgin childhood feeling that was not easily going to be erased. She was more sincere than Judy, straight shooting and non-evasive. It was easier to understand her, and her eyes were always considerate and humble. Stella stuck with him during his most difficult times as a job seeker and at times denying her comfort to cheer him up. That again kept him going. It gave him a sense of worth.

It had not been an easy task breaking the old culture of Manga. The church had dramatically made roads spiritually and culturally. But still there were intercultural suspicions amongst some of the elders. Musa had taken time to convince them of his choice of a wife. He was determined to pioneer in shedding a new light on the village. He had put a spirited argument and finally the elders had allowed him to marry Stella Achieng. Much had changed with Christianity having taken root in the village, and people saw one another as children of God irrespective of their culture and gender. Education was permeating and changing perceptions. One white pastor had even married a local girl in church. "Culture is dynamic, not static," he argued. "What is ideal today may not be ideal tomorrow. Culture is a factor of times. We have to change with world trends for the better," Musa further impressed the elders.

The elders listened to him. He was the most educated in the village. He was their hope and maybe, they reasoned, Musa had learnt something new that they did not know. Some just wondered on the new development and only reserved their comments. They were not amused. One said, "a female dog took a male dog to the lake, meaning, when a man wants to marry, he would look for a bride from anywhere, even from the land of the enemy." But Musa's mother had waited for too long to see her daughter-in-law. All Musa's age mates were long married with their own children. Denying her son this chance and his choice of a wife thus sending him back to the drawing board to look for another girl, was not going to be a wise move. It could only cause more delay in his marriage. She was pious in the church and had seen the light. They were taught in church that all people are children of God.

Stella's qualities sold her well to the village. She made an instant impact the moment she stepped into Manga. She was easily sociable, eager to listen, learn, integrate and she charmed everyone with her sense of humour. She carried a pot and joined the village women in fetching water from the river. She had grown up in Manga, and she understood the people's thinking and way of life. Then Musa's mother would say "better the devil you know than the angel you do not know." She could be heard telling her fellow women, "do not praise a daughter-in-law you have not seen. Accept the one you have. Isn't this the daughter of Onyango who taught our children? Who did not drink water in his house?" Apparently, Stella's family had left behind a positive imprint on the people. "If she has the characteristics of her parents, she will make a wonderful wife," they said.

Many changes had taken place in Manga. Ideally, what were culturally held paramount were developing cracks and were slowly being replaced with emerging blends of culture. A new light was emerging to all, even to the elders. It was no secret. Not long after, several new churches had sprout all over the ranges of Manga. The bells rang in the morning and in the evening calling the villagers for worship. Many people from all over the country had come there to preach. The missionaries preached that God created all people equal in His own image and likeness. They called the villagers to repent and be saved. The message had infused into many people's hearts. Many villagers had been drawn in, and many had endeavoured to change their ways and hearts. This change had greatly contributed to softening the hearts of the elders to allow for the intertribal marriages, and embraced education with belated vengeance.

Stella and Musa's happiness was consummate. Both sides had given them the go ahead to tie the knot. Stella's parents had no questions to Stella's request. All they wanted was her to be happy in her new home. Plans for the wedding day were meticulously executed. Friends from both sides came in to assist in the arrangement. The wedding ceremony was only a day away. Musa knew Judy had lost the battle. It was too late for her to turn the tables. He reasoned that the only way for Judy was to look for another man who could accept to be taken for a ride. Not him. No. He was happy with Stella.

Stella and Musa's wedding day was the most hilarious occasion. It was a beautiful ceremony of their life attended by so many friends, relatives and well-wishers. Perhaps it was the first of the kind Stella would vividly remember. The elders of Manga had visited Stella's family in Kisumu to 'see' the home of their daughter-in-law to be. Elders from Kisumu had been invited to Manga. They spent a night of merry making there. A goat was slaughtered for them and beer was drunk from the pot. The dowry was paid. Six cows, a bull and a goat according to the Gusii traditional customs. The goat was to facilitate Stella's mother to bring the first food to Musa's home for his parents and kin, *obokima bw'abaibori n'eamate.*

The church at Kisumu was full that morning with people dressed in very smart suits. Some elders from Manga adorned traditional regalia: hides and monkey caps. To give the wedding a cultural meaning, they carried their spears and shields. Many colourful flowers adorned the church and the road leading to the church. Stella's rural home in Kisumu was decorated and meticulously cleaned.

Stella was happy, indeed very happy, that finally she had won the man she loved and dreamed about. However, she had some misgivings. She was not yet sure of the intricate issues involved in making a really happy home. She wasn't sure, she pondered. Although her mother had taken time to counsel and encourage her, she still somehow felt like a small child in her mother's house and still yearned for her mother's vast experiences in home-making. Stella thought that soon she was to be a wife, a mother and the new responsibilities on her hands elucidated a mixture of feelings. She was half scared and half excited. However, the excitement overrode the fears. She knew she was leaving her beautiful home forever to go and make her own together with her husband. Then, she was parting with her friends to go far away where chances of meeting again were minimal. She found tears flowing down her cheeks unabated: tears of fear, and tears of joy. But again, she knew this was another stage in her life. She had made an inevitable decision and there was no turning back. She did not want these to overwhelm her.

There were intermittent morning showers as the wedding ceremony progressed inside the church. It was good that way. Showers were seen as a blessing to water the germinating seeds of a new life. Stella and Musa were the germinating seeds and showers were a good sign that their wedding had been blessed and accepted by God.

A number of people had attended the wedding. Most remarkably absent was Judy. Musa knew she was not in Kenya and she had not been invited. Had she been in the country, Musa was not sure whether she could have honoured the invitation. He could not fathom her reaction. Regardless, there was no turning back. The congregation sang in unison a Kiswahili chorus as the bridal party of maids, page boys and flower girls dressed similarly in pink clothes and matched slowly synchronizing their movements with the pianist to the altar. Stella, bridegroom and the congregation waited in anticipation. The pianist played a familiar tune and the congregation sang along. "*Bwana akaona si vizuri mme awe peke yake, akamuumba msaidizi, yeye ndiye bibi...,* God saw it not good for a man to be alone. He gave him a wife as a helper."

There was loud applause, ululations, drumming and horning. The pastor conducted the wedding with charisma. Stella and Musa took their marriage vows as the congregation cheered them. Cheers and songs filled the air. Every face lit up with a smile. Stella was bursting with joy that was contagious and tears of joy flowed down her cheek when finally Musa slipped a golden ring onto her finger. It was one of her happiest moments of her life. Even the cake Musa fed her that day did not mean more than this. "Let not man put asunder what God has joined," the pastor said.

Outside the church, Stella could see women and young girls singing happily:

Suiti Suiti banana
Egetenga kie ritoke
Suiti suiti banana
Egetenga kie ritoke

Stella ase oragende
Ondikere rirube
Stella ase oragende
Ondikere rirube

Suiti suiti Nyarogendo
Ebasi Nyarogendo
Suiti suiti Nyorogendo
Ebasi Nyagetiro

Sweet sweet banana
The sweet bunch of bananas
Sweet Sweet banana
The sweet bunch of bananas

Stella wherever you go
Send me a letter
Stella wherever you go
Send a letter

Sweet sweet *Nyagetiro*
The bus for the hills
Sweet sweet *Nyagetiro*
The bus for the hills

On the other side, the bridal party, page boys and friends were happily dancing, singing and ululating:

Ee uu
Sore my dear
Eng'ombe nyamagoro ane
Sore my dear
Nero yang'ura uu
Sore my dear

Ee friend
Sorry my dear
The four legged cow
Sorry my dear
Has stolen my friend
Sorry my dear

They were joined by Musa's father and his uncle, elder Nyakundi. They were all dancing and gyrating their hips, backs and shoulders. Then elder Nyakundi was heard saying, "indeed times have changed. All people are God's people. Stella is now my daughter."

The pastor took time to share with them ingredients that would make their marriage better. He enumerated love for each other, mutual respect, faithfulness and open communication as inevitable ingredients to a successful marriage. Stella and Musa were determined to fulfill their marriage vows. Stella was confident that Fred, as she fondly called Musa, would fill her heart with unending delight. She was determined to go and give her very best in all circumstances.

After the wedding, Stella and Musa proceeded to Mombasa for their honeymoon. They needed time to be together alone and away from home to ponder over the occasion. They had saved well for the wedding, and the pre-wedding party had raised some reasonable money.

Coast was exciting. It was the first time in their lives they spent luxuriously eating and sleeping in expensive hotels and visiting exciting resorts and historical sites in a hired vehicle. Special occasions come once in a lifetime. They argued. They were determined to make the best of their wedding. They were not going to wed again. The presence of many white tourists spiced their honeymoon. It was a December holiday when Europe experienced winter and many white tourists came to Africa to escape the cold season.

In the evening of the twenty-fourth of December, Stella and Musa sat in their double suite hotel room in the White Sand Beaches Hotel watching early evening news. It was the eve of the Christmas and the Christmas mood was in the air. They were to spend their Christmas holiday at the coast, then fly back to Nairobi. The bulletin took them aback when the news brief was read. The news reader had read, "Prohibited drugs worth millions of shillings impounded at the airport." It went on, "a Kenyan woman in her mid-twenties was arrested this morning at Jomo Kenyatta International Airport with a consignment of narcotic drugs with a street value of millions of shillings. The drugs, among them heroin and cocaine, were packed in mini-sachets weighing fifty grams each in one full carton of ten kilograms. These drugs were presented as paracentamols destined to RM Pharmaceuticals Company Ltd, a local Pharmaceutical company dealing in drug importation. Initial leads had led to the arrest of a young woman by the name Judith Nyachera Makosa. The narcotic police believe that she is in a ring of well-connected and influential drug barons and foreign anti-establishment persons with an aim to dis...There was a total black out in the room.

"Did I hear right?" Musa inquired in a surprised tone.

"Yes, you did," she said. "I heard clearly Judith Nyachera Makosa. There could be no other with those names."

"It cannot be," Musa interjected. "It's unbelievable. Judy? Dealing in prohibited drugs? No!"

There was silence in the room apart from the buzzing

of the notorious coastal mosquitoes and the occasional murmur of the towering coconut trees outside. Musa stood up from his chair and wobbled in the dark to the window and stared into the dimly lit night. Cold sea breezes blew in gently. The moon was slowly surging up. The Indian ocean was just across. His eyes stretched far to the smoky ocean. The sea waves rolled back onto themselves sending icy bubbles into the misty and salty air.

Power resumed once again, and the whole place was fully lit. Musa walked back and sat on the edge of the sofa, and then stared at Stella who was sitting on the same sofa. Stella was deep in thought. Musa was calm.

"If I'm not dreaming, I truly pity her," he said, "and now I understand the source of her affluence."

Stella responded with a nod then said, "I know Judy. She grew up an upright girl. Perhaps it is somebody else," she tried to reassure herself.

Chapter Sixteen

Judith's arrest was covered in all the local dailies. The story was on the front pages making the arrest the talk of the day. Beside the arrest story was a picture of a relatively well-built and expensively dressed beautiful young woman with her face partially hidden by the inner side of her arm. Two police women stood next to her. Below the picture was the name Judith Nyanchera Makosa. She had already admitted to have been in possession of the consignment where the drugs were found. She was on her way back from the U.K. The drugs were worth millions of shillings. However, she had said the consignment belonged to her friend of the British nationality known as Richard Morgans. Morgans was due to fly in the next morning. She would be charged in court with possession and trafficking of the prohibited drugs contrary to Cap 245 of the laws of Kenya.

The early evening news further reported that the anti-narcotics police were following leads to arrest more suspects who were connected to Judith. With her arrest the police were definitely going to unearth and break the underground world of influential drug traffickers, an organization they believed Judy belonged to. Their aim was obvious: to make illegal money irrespective of the consequences the drugs posed. The main targets were school children. They did not care about the aftermath, the brains the drug would smash to garbage, the able bodied youth they would crash to papers, the ill health they would inflict in society, the millions of shillings that would go to treatment of drug related diseases, the soaring crime rate as a result of drug related influence, and the economic draw back the country would realize.

Stella and Musa read the arrest story with deep concern and sympathy for Judy. They pitied her. Judy was Stella's classmate in secondary schools and a close friend. She had been Musa's fiancée, a fact that Stella knew. Musa recalled the last moment he had coincidentally met Judy in the street of Nairobi. It was not the Judy he had known all those years ago. She exuded greater confidence and a scent of affluence. She drove an expensive limousine, lived in the exclusive upper market, Runda, and was managing to settle her bills. It was evident that luck, which had lurked somewhere unknown, had finally visited Judy in a big way. But then, he realized that he was cheating himself. Perhaps with the arrest, the truth had finally come out. It was a pity that the innocent-looking Judy had gotten herself involved in shoddy deals in an endeavour to make a quick dollar, which has now put her in a precarious and embarrassing situation. Even with the harsh reality of the city as a job seeker, she had no greater reason to be involved in this business. He reasoned.

Until lately, the law on the offenders involved in narcotic drugs was not that harsh. Suspects could be fined, acquitted or jailed for a few years, even months or given some remedial punishment. With the global outcry on the increase of the illegal narcotic drug trafficking and the obvious dangers they were posing, it had necessitated that parliament reviewed the law. Parliamentarians argued that if the law was not tightened to discourage and seal the loopholes used by the drug dealers and peddlers, then the youths, the nation's future and hope who were always easy targets to these drugs, were at risk. In short, the nation was losing its war on socio-economic development and losing a sizeable generation to the drugs. The bill was anonymously passed to become a law. Henceforth, any person found to be in possession of any prohibited drug, as small as a roll of *Cannabis Sativa* was to receive a minimum sentence of ten years in jail and possibly a hefty fine. The obvious conviction was that Judy would not escape ten years at minimum if proven guilty.

At the Jomo Kenyatta International Airport, security was tightened. The police waited for a man of British descents, Richard Morgans. Every incoming plane was carefully searched and all passengers carefully scrutinized. Richard Morgans was never arrested. The police asked the Interpol to assist. The Interpol's relentless search for Richard yielded no fruits. Richard was said to be mysterious or existed only in Judy's imagination.

Given the amount of drugs involved and their huge street value, the issue gained mileage. It happened at a time when fingers were pointed to influential politicians and businessmen as the ones who amassed their wealth through drug related businesses. Accusations were traded and countered. These all happened at a time when the country was sinking into drug abuse; when politicians were said to use drugs as a scapegoat to cover up their evils, and when youths were said to be given drugs by influential politicians to disrupt political rallies or unwanted religious meetings thought to have "unpalatable" political agendas; when riots in universities and schools were many and blamed them on drug taking. So the issue on prohibited drugs was on everybody's lips. Politicians took turns to comment on the issue. They condemned prohibited drug taking. They blamed the rich and the corrupt people who always plotted in scandalous activities to enrich themselves at the expense of the masses without a care for the future.

The government issued a statement. It read in part, "those behind the rackets of prohibited narcotics drug trafficking and peddling are well known enemies of development. The government is alert and will do everything possible to bring them to justice. And those with useful information who could assist the police to arrest the culprits are asked to volunteer the information to their nearest police station." He promised that all the information would be treated in great confidence. The public had reservation for the government statement. If they were well known, then why were they not arrested and prosecuted in a court of law?

Back in the village of Borabu, they got the shocking news. It hit the village like a hot bullet and spread like a bush fire in a desert during the hot summer. In no time, it was the talk of the village and on everybody's lips; young and old alike. To many it was like a nightmare. It was scary, sending cold chill down the spine. It was hard to think how the young Judy could survive the notoriety of prison. None in the village had ever been arrested on such or any serious crime. The only arrests they could remember were related to possession of local brews, and usually it was men who were arrested. Not women. The news took time to digest and believe its authenticity, and time for many who heard it to recover from it. Judith's mother, Regina, ran short of breath and collapsed. She had to be resuscitated by the quick action of the villagers.

Many villagers came to comfort the family. Women sat together talking in whispers and tears flowing freely from their already red eyes. They cried with Judy's mother. They comforted her and spent several nights with her in her house. The tradition was that when a villager wept, the whole village wept too. It was an easy way of assisting the afflicted person to dry his or her tears faster. When a child was born, it did not only belong to its parents, it was for all in the society. Judy was a child of Borabu. She was the one of few girls from Borabu who had gone through university and they looked at her as their beacon of hope, the village investment and a role model to the other children.

Judy had always exuded confidence and created trust with her parents and to the whole village. In spite of the fact that many people praised her beauty more than most girls in the village, and she was one of the most educated of all the girls in Borabu, Judy was humble and respectful. These and other qualities had thrust her to heights of respect and created many hopes for the villagers.

Regina had never seen any bad traits in her daughter. She had never stolen, lied to her or done anything to justify serious parental intervention. She was an infallible girl. They had never seen or heard of her drink beer, walk in bad company, or even get involved in any questionable or forbidden movements. She was a girl every other parent envied to be his or her own and always asked their children to emulate. To the villagers, Judy was a role model. She had built in them a strong and firm confidence about her character.

On her last visit to the village, as usual Judy was warm to everybody. She drove her navy Prado to her home with many presents for her mother and the other members of her family. She stopped at every point to greet the villagers. She had told them that the company she was working with, R.M. Pharmaceuticals Ltd, had decided to send her abroad for further training. Her parents were happy that finally, their efforts in educating their daughter had yielded fruits. The company was paying her a handsome salary with a lot of fringe benefits. That was the only information they had of their dear daughter's work.

Daudi, Judy's father, got all sorts of advice from his friends. Some were discouraging, while others were encouraging. However, he was barely able to cope with this sad news. Regina had always been his source of comfort during times of difficulties. He knew the pain she was undergoing. Judy was his first born and he loved her dearly. As a father, he decided that the best option at that moment was to hire a component lawyer to argue their daughter's case in court. It did not matter whether she had messed up or not. Still, Judy was their daughter, the opener and blessing to his family.

Chapter Seventeen

Judy's mother sat outside her house staring at the setting sun to the west. It was evening and the sun was slowly setting behind the hills, casting ghostly long shadows. The valleys were already darker with crickets competing to whistle from their hideouts. The birds chirped merrily as they returned to their nests. She stared straight ahead pensively. A few metres away, her two grade cows foraged on a heap of a newly cut napier grass stacked in their zero-grazing unit. She slumped back onto her *makuti*-woven-makeshift chair in dejection, feeling low in spirit and pondering over the fate of her dear daughter, Makosa. Life was not treating her well. Her thoughts were in a total turmoil. She felt completely at a loss. Defeat hovered immensely along her path ruining all chances of her happiness. Judy's arrest had put her family into a great deal of scorn, ridicule and gossip. The family's pride was wasted away into the bones. It was a bitter test.

Suddenly, a lizard emerged from a wall. It made brief stops, making quick stares then moved fast towards an errant fly. It turned its head left and right then swiftly flung its slender red tongue. The poor naughty fly had no chance. A life was lost to sustain another. The presumably happy reptile sleuthed forward for another catch. This time it was not lucky. Never! A hen emerged full speed from a corner with her chicks in hot pursuit knocking the poor lizard on the head several times. And then it continued to enjoy the meal together with her chicks chuckling in dirges. The hen was to be the meal for the family in a few days, and the food chain would go on. She watched these incidences quietly. These were the only moments when her mind was peaceful.

Memories of her past cropped up. They were fresh in her mind as if it was a movie she had just watched, or as if it was only yesterday. When she was married to Daudi, then a senior government clerk, she was a young beautiful and charming girl, full of life and high expectations. Many young men had flocked her home seeking her hand in marriage, but she turned them all down. But when Daudi emerged, it was like he had come from the moon. She had to throw away all her pride and dreams to marry him. Then, she had expected a Cinderella type of marriage. She wanted to live happily ever after. Unfortunately this was not the case, especially in their initial years of marriage. It was long into her marriage when her womb was blessed with their first child, Judith Nyanchera Makosa, whom she affectionately named after her late grandmother Makosa, her mentor and pride of her life.

Makosa had acted like her mother. Regina had grown up and spent most of her early years at her grandmother's house, fetching water and firewood for her, listening to her sweet endless stories and songs, and sleeping beside her come the evenings. Makosa had played a leading role in her upbringing. And even when she was getting married, she had literally moved from her grandmother's house and not her mother's house. Given this scenario, Regina had great attachment to Makosa. When Makosa was so sick, six years after Regina's marriage, and it was evident that she was spending her last days, she had sent for Regina, "go, tell her to come," she had requested in a feeble voice with her teeth clinched, "so that she can see me as I die."

Regina had gone quickly to find her frail body in a mat, virtually unable to talk. When she saw Regina through her misty and faint eyes, she had barely managed to talk. She stretched her frail arm, held Regina's palm, spat on it and fumbled softly, "don't give up my daughter. Do not be discouraged by the adversity of life. Do not." She repeated. "Do not forget me. Our god and ancestors have heard your cries and seen your tears. When you get a child, call her Makosa. Then I shall live longer to the next generations." Two days later, Makosa slept peacefully never to wake up again. She joined the world of ancestors at an advanced age. She was ninety. Regina had wept bitterly and spent many days mourning her grandma.

Most people had believed that Regina was barren. They gossiped behind her back. "Ten years is too long." Some thought that she had been bewitched, while others whispered behind her back that a bad omen had befallen her. She had intentionally put off the ceremonial fire when she was circumcised and she had not bothered to be cleansed. "No," others said, "The daughter of the chief was only reaping the fruits of her father. Did the father not invite curses to himself by being too brutal to his subjects? Unless she was cleansed, no child would come from her womb." Despite all these talks, Daudi stood with her and showered her with love and understanding in abundance. This gave her strength and spirit to continue.

Many people advised Daudi to take up another wife who could give him children and make him complete and respectable. They argued that a man without children was a tree without roots and hence no future. One man offered to give him his daughter free without paying pride price. However, Daudi always stood by Regina. They explained to him in detail that there was nothing wrong to marry two women. His father had two and his grandfather had several. Others wondered why he could not divorce Regina and marry a woman who could bear him children. "When a tree does not bear fruits, it is usually cut down, uprooted and one that bears fruits planted on its place," they argued. "A woman is like a pot placed on a hole. Once the contents are drained, it is removed and in its place taken by a pot with full beer." Some said that Regina had bought a love potion from a witch-doctor and fed it to Daudi. Hence Daudi could not see her barrenness. This explained why he could not think of marrying a woman who could bear him children. How else could they explain the reason why a man with two eyes could continue clinging to a sinking boat? Once he was gone, who could carry his spear and shield, and sit on his stool? They reasoned.

Daudi listened to these talks, but only laughed. He continued to shower his love to Regina. Though he also cherished the idea of having children by Regina, she remained fulfilling in his dreams. She was his source of comfort, inspiration and intimacy. She always filled his heart with joy none could do. Her charms were ruthlessly irresistible. He knew that children were a product of marriage but not always a happy one. They were a blessing that were to come at a later date, God willing. As a staunch Christian, he knew that God's blessing could come at any time. Sarah, Abraham's wife, had given birth to Isaac at an old age when they had given up. Daudi had accepted Regina's weakness. Regina had refused all other men in order to marry her sweetheart. Was that not a reason enough to be proud of? On their wedding day, they had made solemn vows before the priest that their marriage was to weather storms. It was for better or for worse, in sickness or in health, till death does them apart. Daudi had remained faithful to these vows.

Regina had become a staunch Christian. She prayed faithfully to God to open her womb, just as he did for Sarah. Special prayers were offered in their house, in crusades and in virtually all Christian meetings Regina and Daudi attended. They visited many reputable hospitals and doctors who confirmed to them that there was nothing medically wrong to cause them to worry. They were given fertility drugs and advised to keep up an active marital life and then wait for the fruits that were children. Months passed into years. This reinforced their fear of witchcraft or even having wronged some supreme being.

Daudi was promoted. This meant some more income. Through these earnings he hired a shop which Regina ran to keep her busy and to further improve their income. This occupied her, momentarily forgetting what she was going through.

As the saying goes, "if you are looking for a deer and you cannot find it up the hill, try it down the hill." In the eighth year of her marriage the pressure from friends and relatives had become unbearable. Regina lived in mortal fear of dying childless. She now became optimistic that what modern medicine had failed to offer, traditional herbalist could offer. Regina and Daudi started trying their luck with herbalists and witch-doctors. They traversed the whole country looking for a healer anywhere. One weekend they could be in the coast seeing a renowned magician or herbalist and the next in Nyanza. Anyone they heard who could heal a woman or a couple unable to bear children was tried. They were in a state of utter desperation. The healers advanced all sorts of theories. "You have been bewitched, a work of jealousy and bad eyed people," some barely prescribed. Others advised them to give sacrifices to some supreme beings in order to be cleansed of the evil spirits.

They offered various sacrifices of animals. They took different types of herbal concoctions. They ate different types of food. They were given magical charms to chase away evil eyes around them. In some cases, fingers were pointed to some of the neighbours and relatives who were said to empathize with them by day but bewitched them by night. In one way or another they were responsible for their predicaments. They had secretly held Regina's womb for some strange reasons. The herbalists seemingly took advantage of their desperation to charge them high fees. However, they were determined to give anything to remove the blemish they termed as inflicted disgrace. They had given all sorts of sacrifices, but nothing had changed.

They were spending all the money they could lay their hands on and they were getting poorer and poorer every day. In this sad situation they had given up trying and let everything rest at that while fate took its own course. As if that was the prescription in waiting, Regina had conceived a year later. Joy made her face glow brighter. She cared for the pregnancy like a little egg on hand. This marked the end of her long, slow and anxious years of waiting.

When the pregnancy began to show, many people reacted differently. "It cannot be true. It is not real," some said. "See, ten years is long. She must be playing games," they urged. "You know nowadays if a woman cannot get a child she can wrap pieces of clothes round her tummy to fake a pregnancy. After nine months she can buy or steal a baby." Some people whispered behind Regina and Daudi's backs. Nevertheless, when the baby was finally born, those who doubted were proved wrong. The baby took after her father with impunity and her mother in every respect: in colour and in smile to everybody's satisfaction. Their house was for once full of people. Friends and relatives streamed in with presents for the miracle baby.

Regina named her Judith Nyanchera Makosa and was fondly called Judy by friends and relatives alike. The name Judith reminded Regina of her school teacher whom she greatly admired and she had wanted to be like. She was ever smart with a good command of language. She wore clean, well iron dresses. Nyanchera, meaning a pathway, reminded her of the pain she underwent for many years, traversing the country in search of a cure, before Judy was finally born, and the ridicule she endured in the eyes of many, being labelled barren, when indeed she had a fertile womb. Makosa was her late grandmother. This was in memory of her; it was the fulfillment of the late Makosa's wish. A dream that finally became true.

With the birth of Judy, Regina's life changed its course, acquired a new meaning and status in society. It brought in a lot of joy. Regina and Daudi could now laugh freely. Nobody could gossip, mock and laugh at them behind their backs. Regina was not barren after all. Their disgrace had been washed away into the bones.

Briefly, that is how Judy was born. She was a miracle child born at a time when she was least expected: at a moment of great need. Later, Regina had given birth to five other children without any problems, three boys and two more girls. Of them all, Judy was her pearl, the blessings and opener of her womb, a womb that had been locked in mystery.

Regina wondered where she had gone wrong as a mother. Not too long ago, she had taken seriously her advisory role as a mother in guiding her daughter on matters of life. She spent time with Judy telling her to tread carefully through the mucky waters of life. She advised her to relate carefully and navigate wisely in her undertakings, and not all that glitters is gold. Had she failed to instill discipline in her? Was it another great test she was facing? Had God abandoned her? She did not have answers to all her tormenting questions. Yet, she was comforted that God had a great plan for her. Regina vowed to stand by her daughter; to defend her to the last ounce of energy as a gesture a beloved daughter and as testimony to unfailing love of a mother.

Chapter Eighteen

The small cubicle serving as a remand was pitch dark with a small window high up the wall, allowing in some light and fresh air. For the six months Judy had been in custody, it had been a nightmare. An awful and nauseating stench emitted from the toilet at a corner. It choked her nostrils. The bed bugs and the lice scrawling on the floor day and night were a scare. The tough and ruthless prison wardens and the hardened seasoned inmates who had no heart of mercy for new inmates made life harder. To her, this was the most petrifying and hair-raising encounter in her life. The present appeared to be held captive by the past full of promising hopes and a future locked and hidden in mysteries.

Initially, Judy had refused to eat. The incident embarrassed her. Further, the food was sulkily raw and lacking in taste. Raw boiled beans and *ugali* popularly known as *zima* and broken cabbage were the popular meal for supper and lunch. When she realized that she would die of hunger, she had slowly started eating until she got used to food, in the remand. She had considered it unpalatable. Even in these conditions, there was a general feeling that prison reforms had made the remand a better place. In that small room holding twelve suspects, each had her own charges. Some were minor charges ranging from being in possession of illicit liquor, *changaa*, loitering at odd hours, to more serious charges of theft and murder. There were young girls of her age and older women in the age bracket of her mother. Some appeared to be in the wrong place. They were dignified and reserved, distant and contemplative, while there were the seasoned hard-core types who felt at home in these conditions.

All of them had their own stories to tell. They teased, laughed and amused one another with endless poignant stories. These stories were repeated now and again when new ones were not forthcoming, and overtime a story was narrated, it carried new tastes and flavours to it as if it had never been told. They kept them company, and momentarily helped them drift from the bitter reality of their misgivings. Surprisingly, some were happier to be in there than being free where life was harsh and difficult. Thanks to Hon Moody Awori who instituted prison reforms when he was Vice President and Minister for Home Affairs. These reforms had given a human face in the remands and other corrective centres. They could laugh as they switched from topic to topic. Those who were married missed their husbands and the serenity of their homes, while the unmarried longed too to see their children and their boyfriends. One woman, though married, was in for the wrong reason. She had broken the "home fence", she said, to entertain a secret lover, *mpango wa kando*, a risky venture. Another was in for having scalded her husband's "side dish," as she called her husband's lover and secretary. Time had greatly changed the values of society from a traditional one.

At night when everybody was tired and asleep, Judy could drift to the days gone. As she grew up, she was a darling to her parent's, given the nature of her birth. Life was butter and bread. If she cried for a piece of bread, two loaves of bread were bought. If she coughed a little, that was enough to raise a serious concern on her state of health and her parents reacted to it with unnecessary tenacity. Any small complaint she made of any mistreatment, her mother acted swiftly with stern warnings to whoever was the supposed offender. Even as the other children were born into the family, the situation had not changed much. Her requests were met immediately. Even as she grew up, she was still treated with the delicacy of a young child. She was showered with beautiful expensive presents and encouraging praises from aunts, uncles, friends and her parents. They called her special names. Judith, Nyanchera, Makosa, Nana, Baba, Mum, Moikiri one, my beloveth, you name it. She was allocated special, and less strenuous duties. Despite this kind of treatment, she had ironically grown respectful, intelligent and as a beautiful as her mother, "unequal" and unmatched with any other girl in the in the city and the village.

Judy's affair with Harry Mambo had begun quite unexpectedly. She observed. She had heard of bosses who took advantage of young vulnerable girls looking for jobs. She learnt this first hand when she had gone to Harry's office for an interview. Harry kept on sending sweet smiles to her as they discussed the prospects of a job. Appearing courteous, he invited her for lunch. She grumbled on whether to accept the offer or not. Perhaps, this was part of the interview, she reasoned. Naïve, she accepted the offer.

Harry led her to his posh Mercedes Benz, opened the door for her, drove her to an exclusive restaurant in the outskirts of the city and order red wine for her sumptuous meal. This became a routine. She learnt that though Harry was an old man of her father's age, he wasn't as bad a person as she had initially thought. She got hooked on seeing him now and again in his office. Harry gave her expensive presents of jewellery and designer clothes and pocket money to last her several days. It augmented the money she received from Richard. They had many outings outside the city.

These many visits had led from one thing to the other, a cup of coffee in a posh restaurant, a bottle of wine and finally an amorous affair. In the initial stage, she did not mind it as the prospects of a job and scaling the ladder lasted. After all, she could reason, it was no secret some girls in college did the same. Was she not a woman like them? Her morals had been eroded by the harsh reality as a job seeker. As time went on, she became discontent and scared when she realized that a job was not forthcoming, yet the many outings with Harry had taught her a lesson or two. Being a graduate job seeker with big dreams, she had to use the powers as a woman to survive and mint money.

Judy had witnessed her cousin, young and innocent, Millie get pregnant and drop out of school in the name of fun and love with a man old enough to be her father. Somehow, this reinforced her fear of the high price she could pay for her adventures and expeditions. Then there was the real fear of HIV and AIDS. She realized that Harry had a hidden agenda for her: to ravage her youth for his own pleasure. She wasn't ready to bear the scars of painful memories or to be a second wife as Harry was putting it to her. She decided to move on and dedicate her time to Richard who always promised her the world and beyond while exploring other promising avenues.

In a few months of meeting Richard, Judy drove her own Toyota Corolla, a present from Richard on her birthday. Richard was a seasoned tourist to Kenya. He came with a lot of money to spend, to have fun and Judy made herself available for him any time he was around. She enjoyed his company too. As a young girl and a young man, the horizon appeared far and beyond. Only Richard and his money could help her scale the walls to riches.

When Richard was away in London, Judy needed company to give her fun and good time, to fill the missing link. City life was easy for a young beautiful woman looking for some adventure and fun. All one needed to do was to make herself attractive and available. Pose as a professional and meet the right team. Fatima had taught her the tricks. Her natural beauty gave her an extra advantage over the other girls. She knew how to strike it. In her job seeking adventure, she came to know prominent lawyers, businessmen, academicians and men who held positions of influence. Men openly fought for her, wars that tore the hearts, skins and killed reputations.

Judy thought that she had known Richard well and known the type of business he did. Indeed, she had had a suspicion that whatever she delivered were not normal drugs. No office to run the business, the places and hours she delivered the drugs, the unkempt, shrewd customers, and the secrecy with which the business was run were all pointers that something was a mess. She was naïve and greedy for money. The truth was slowly unfolding and it was hard to believe after all those promises, the fun and good times they had had together. She realized that she knew little or almost nothing about him. For instance, she did not know that he dealt in prohibited drugs. If she had known in advance, she would have never associated with him, at least not to that extent. She never realized that she was being used as a conduit for evil.

Yes; Richard had given her a shoulder to lean on in the harsh environment as a jobseeker. He had hired a house for her, given her all the money she required and exclusive big cars, one after the other in a short time. In addition, she had a fat account at her relatively young age. The only important duty she did to Richard was to deliver drug consignments to various people in the city. Her house also acted as a store for his drugs. She was made to believe they were for medical use, not prohibited.

Fatima and Calvin were regular visitors to her house. They acted as his sales persons to the retail markets. Sometimes she delivered the drugs directly to Calvin's house. The same people she had delivered the drugs to had stood in court in her presence and denied ever associating or ever knowing her. Even Fatima had denied her. Now she stood alone to be nailed to the cross while the real culprits, Richard and his accomplices were safe, hiding and enjoying the fortunes she had ignorantly assisted in making. Yes, they had a wonderful time together and what resembled love had flourished like a tree planted by a river side. She became even more aware that Richard had really taken advantage of her naivety. She remember the saying "regrets are like grandchildren. They come long after the events." And this was now true in her case.

Judy focused back into her childhood ambitions probably shattered forever. She had wanted to become a doctor, more specifically, a gynecologist to assist women unable to have children. When she qualified for economics, she took it with gusto. She excelled and looked forward for better things. Now, her future appeared locked in an abyss. She realized how naïve and greedy for life she had been. How the scandal had dented her image and that of her once revered family. She felt stupid and sorry for herself and more so for her family. She realized how she had offended her God, her mother, and her love, Musa, the only man who had really promised her more than she could see then. But her selfish strive and ignorant approach to life had stood between them, and shattered her future. She felt she could go mad, and wished that she could turn back time and be given a new beginning. Then she would put the record straight. Given this chance, she would not allow the Richards' or the Fatimas' to influence her life. Had she not followed Fatima's enticement blindly, she would not have ended up like this. "What does Richard mean?" She asked herself banging the wall. She felt that one day she would get hold of his neck for revenge.

Judy felt miserably hollow. As painful memories pursued her from the past, clinging more stubborn to her sub-conscious. They were driving her crazy. Bitterness of that cheat, and her belated innocent approach to life betrayed her, leaving her weary and hopelessly defeated. She closed her eyes and prayed to be freed, to start life all over again with determination to achieve her dreams and to succeed. When she opened them she felt a calm inside her that no money or love could buy. It promised riches, peace and wonders beyond. The prayer helped her to overcome many unfounded fears that had compounded to weaken her further.

She seemed to hear her mother singing slowly and softly, her usual favourite song in an evening like this while busy in the kitchen and telling her, "Makosa, my Makosa, go home, my daughter, go home to my mother. Take this millet. Go home tell my mother and father not to forget me, their daughter." Again Judy would hear her mother telling her again. "Do not disappoint me, your mother. Your humble reward for me is to see you grow up disciplined, happy and successful in your endeavours." And Judy would obediently answer, "Yes mother." She heard the echoes of promises of yester-years ringing again and again. "Yes mama, I'll endeavour to fulfill your request. I won't let you down," she could promise.

From the debris of these shattered hopes and dreams rose a ray of hope for a better future. Judy fell back on her mat and slumped into a quiet contemplation. In her sleep, she saw herself happily married with her own children practicing her childhood dream, gynecology. Then one evening, she was alone in an unfamiliar place walking home from church with her Bible in one hand and her bag on the other. She walked through a footpath winding through a thicket full of thorns and mucky soil. Then suddenly, a strange looking animal appeared from the thicket. It was half man and half lion. Evidently it was ugly, fierce and strong, but maintained a silly sarcastic smile. "Come," it said, "I'm your best friend and I shall offer you life everlasting." She started running through the thicket, jumping over the tall grass, but her feet were dragging into the mucky soils. Finally, Judy came across a fast flowing river. She stopped to ponder over the next best move to make. Now the beast was a few metres away with its mouth fully opened, and its thick mane menacingly raised covering most of its neck. If she did not act fast then she was surely food for the beast and her future gone with the wind. She seemed to hear the beast pray, "Lord, I give thanks for this meal which thou have provided."

Judy closed her eyes and jumped into the fast flowing river. It was better to drown than to be torn into pieces by this ugly and fierce creature. Her Bible and bag were swept down by the water current. She screamed as she struggled to swim across the river against the strong currents.

"Judy! Judy!" called out one inmate as she pushed her violently to wake up. "What is happening? You don't want us to sleep?"

Judy turned as she rubbed her eyes to clear them of sleep. She was shaking, "I was drowning in a river," She explained. "I've defeated the beast."

"Which river were you drowning in?" Another inmate inquired sarcastically.

"Where is the beast?" the inmates asked in unison laughing. They knew she had been dreaming.

"Yesterday, you were running after a girl who had stolen your ring meant for your boyfriend. Your dreams appear endless," another interjected.

"Leave her alone. She is a dreamer," an elderly in-mate added her voice.

Judy slowly became aware that she had had a bad dream. She was internally disturbed. This was a third consecutive dream in a week. The dreams reflected on her life and hung incomplete. It was her life which was being pursued by many troubles. The same way the riddles hung incomplete, Judy knew that her future too hung in the balance.

Chapter Nineteen

The proceedings of Judy's case took almost two years with many unnecessary intermittent breaks. One day, it was the magistrate who was unwell, or the prosecutor who was away attending important duties. The effects were unnecessary delays and massive psychological torture. That is how the wheel of justice rolled.

Through her lawyer, Judy had denied all the charges labelled against her. The lawyer had requested the court to release her on a bond to argue her case from outside remand, but the prosecutor protested strongly against that. He argued, "Your Honour, the case before the court is a special one. It touches on the security of the state and affects two friendly countries, Kenya and Britain. I'll draw your attention on the global war on narcotic drugs and their trafficking. Kenya is a member state against trading, trafficking or consumption of prohibited drugs. The effects these drugs cause to our society for the selfish gains of a few crooked individuals like this woman here must be taken into account. This cannot go on unchecked. The world is watching to see how the matter is handled. Bailing her out may put in jeopardy our good relationships with our friendly countries, Britain included, on how we are committed to stamp out the vice. They would interpret that we are not taking serious the war on prohibited drugs. Secondly, Your Honour, the suspect is a citizen of this country while the other one jointly charged with her but not before the court is not a citizen of this country. If she is bailed out, then there is fear she might influence the investigation or abscond. Drug barons and baronesses have lots of money to do anything. It is no secret the amount of money the drugs generate. And very few men and women would not fail to look the other way if greased rightly."

Judy's lawyer defended her vehemently and competently. He refuted that the case touched on the security of the state or even put to jeopardy Kenya's relations with Britain or in any way negated the war against narcotic substances. What did a young girl of Judy's age have to do with security, and how was it to affect the two countries? The case had to be treated as it was. In accordance with the law, Judy was innocent until proven guilty. He accused the prosecution of malice and unprofessionalism. To him it was just like any other proceeding that was being twisted and given a political overtone, probably to settle old scores. He informed the court that the prosecutor was an old acquaintance of the accused and the honourable thing to do was disqualify himself from leading the prosecutions. However, this was not granted nor did the prosecutor disqualify himself.

The lawyer further argued that the accused acted out of the normal African courtesy and hospitality by extending a helping hand to her white friend Richard Morgans, carrying the consignment on his behalf without knowing that the contents were indeed prohibited drugs. If she had known it, she would not have accepted, let alone associate with the culprit given her strong religious background. "Your Honour, my client is a devout Christian," the lawyer remarked. "Her actions were like that of a friend assisting another one to carry a basket to the market without necessarily knowing the contents in the basket. Judith is a young girl with a bright future ahead. The honourable thing was to show her the way, build her, but not destroy her."

The magistrate ruled that Judy could not be bonded. Thus the prosecution won round one. Judy had to go to remand for the next six months to wait for the commencement of her hearing. And when the hearing began, the prosecution called twelve witnesses: The airport police officers, the cleaners, the cloakroom attendants who were on duty that day of arrest, the anti-narcotics police investigators, Fatima and Calvin. Boxes of the prohibited drugs were displayed in court as exhibits. Their evidences were mercilessly ruthless to the defense. They were piercing and brutal. Fatima and Calvin denied any association or ever knowing Judy. It was a matter of saving their flesh.

The hearing went on continuously for two weeks and two days and in the end Judy was more drained from the proceedings than anything else. Finally, the day of reckoning arrived. It was judgement day. It would determine whether Judy would walk free back to the streets of Nairobi, or remain behind bars for a long time.

It was a Monday morning. The weather was foggy and drizzling. A misty air filled the courtroom, and Judy stood pensively and uneasily at the dock guarded by a uniformed police woman. She waited for her fate that now loosely hung on a tight string. The courtroom was filled to capacity with family members, friends and sympathizers. The media was present and sat on all available spaces. Many more were standing in and outside the court room. Musa and Stella sat at a front bench near the dock. Judy's future was evidently hidden somewhere. But the family was happy and somehow confident in the way Judy's defense lawyer had argued her case with enthusiasm and professionalism. He had demanded a high fee and was said to be quite effective behind the scenes in influencing the bench. So, more money had been given to him for this reason. It was not a secret that the judiciary had been penetrated with all sorts of vices: corruption, nepotism, tribalism, indiscipline, and even politics. Justice was said to be up for grabs, and an accused would walk free even when there was overwhelming evidence if the bench was influenced or 'greased' properly. Often, the innocent would find themselves hounded to jail for the same reasons.

Judy wore a frown. She looked weak and emaciated. Her once round and succulent cheeks had sunken, her face wrinkled and her hair was kinky. Evidently, she was internally disturbed and exhausted. Fear was written all over her face. She feared for her future. How would she ever face the people she knew and put the record straight? She felt completely bruised and torn into irreparable pieces with her life surrounded by a mixture of pain and hope, but which hope? That the future might be considerate and understanding to her? She avoided any eye contact with everybody. She felt ashamed. Instead, she preferred to stare on the ground throughout. How could she ever face the same people she had promised so much? The same people she felt she had terribly wronged? The people she had made to believe that she was a perfect girl? The people who had sacrificed for her comfort and who thought that she was their beacon of hope for the younger generation? Then there was her mother, who fondly called her Nyanchera or Makosa and almost adored her.

Judy was aware that the magistrate and the prosecutor were in the same class at the law school. In her adventure for fun and 'good time', she had met them on many occasions and played them the spoiled girl's games. Her adventures had torn skins, bruised hearts, and spawned careers. Each of them had a story about her. The two had once fought over her. Even with that, could they be a hope in this case now that they knew her? She wondered.

The case before her carried a minimum of ten year and a maximum of life sentence without an option of a fine. Further, all properties acquired using drug trafficking money could be seized and forfeited to the state if enough proof was made available to the court that indeed, they were acquired through the ill-gotten money.

Finally, the court was quiet. The magistrate read his judgement for almost an hour uninterrupted. It was long, and detailed. Part of it read, "given the evidence adduced before this court by the witnesses and the police who arrested Judith Nyanchera Makosa on the 24th of December at Jomo Kenyatta International Airport (J.K.I.A) with a consignment of the prohibited drugs, exhibits 1a, 1b.....10k, contrary to cap 245 of the laws of Kenya, the court finds the evidences solidly credible. The court believes that the man by the names Richard Morgans alleged to be the owner of the goods and of British nationality does not exist, as he could not be traced even with the assistance of the International police (Interpol). The court is of the opinion that his naming was an infertile attempt to derail the court from establishing the truth. Further, the defense could not prove beyond reasonable doubt that the accused was assisting the fictitious Richard Morgans with the load of the drugs without her knowledge of the contents in them. The fact that she was arrested with the drugs and admitted to the same, argues itself true to the court's findings. Not knowing the contents in the boxes is no excuse in a court of law. The law states that ignorance of the law is no defense in a court of law." He paused for a glass of water. There was total silence. A pin could drop and be heard a while away.

"To act as a deterrent measure to others who may want to involve themselves in such businesses," he read, "the court must act firmly. The country cannot sit and watch the society fall into drugs, and drug related crimes soaring up and crashing the health, minds and careers of its innocent children. The stability and growth of this nation depends on how sober the minds of its citizens are." He dropped the final bombshell which detonated loudly and clearly. "In view of these, the court adjudges that Judith Nyanchera Makosa is guilty of the offence of being in possession and trafficking of the prohibited drugs contrary to the narcotic drugs and psychotropic substances control act cap 245 of the laws of Kenya. The court considers that she is a first time offender and sentences her to ten years imprisonment without option of a fine. She has fourteen days to appeal. The court adjourns."

The last sentence was drowned in wails and sobs. Judy's mother was carried out of the court room. She cried uncontrollably. Her father's face was covered in dripping sweat. A father's love for his daughter, his beacon of hope, was put to great test. "Ten years, yes, ten years is too long. And she is a first time offender? Ironically she is a first offender," he murmured to himself.

Before Judy was led away from the dock by two police women to a green prison Land Cruiser parked outside the court entrance, she waved goodbye to the stunned crowd. Some waved back consolingly while others stared at her in tears sobbing and wailing. She demonstrated her last patch of courage many couldn't have had at a trying moment like this. She turned around and looked towards Musa and Stella. Musa was staring at her wondering why she had to do what she did. Everybody was staring at her with questioning eyes, may be for the last time for so many years to come. She tried to compose herself. She wasn't crying. She had already cried in remand, tears that could fill the seas and oceans. Judy stared at Musa and then at Stella for a moment, with those appealing and imploring looks, a sign of great remorse was registered on her face. Even with premature wrinkles already forming on her face, courtesy of stress, the radiance of a beautiful girl was ingrained in her forever. With each of them she had shared a memorable past. She was Stella's roommate and a great companion in high school. She was Musa's fiancée, or so she thought. She wished that time was a clock that she could adjust back, then be allowed a moment of kissing her Musa, a man who only let her down when money counted. But money was not all, she reasoned.

Judy's face was in a contortion of hopes unrealized and many dreamed shattered. She tried to open her mouth twice to speak, but she did not. Something seemed to impede her effort. Then with all the determination of a wounded lion in her last breath, she spoke softly and articulately as she always did, with feelings piercing deeper into the heart of a stubborn pharaoh. Radiating charms of the days gone by and opening up wounds of a broken promises, "my hope and promise, dear Musa, I'm really sorry for the past and for what has happened now. I've hurt you and wronged my parents: particularly mum. Please go home tell my mum that I'm truly sorry. I shall overcome all these. Be patient, for I shall overcome, come back and we shall live happily ever after."

She finished speaking. Those who were near her heard these appealing words. There were rivers of tears that ran down her round cheeks, and down to her alluring breasts. Musa turned to evade Judy's eyes. For a moment he felt like a betrayer. He looked at Stella. She was staring at him with quizzical eyes, in disbelief and astonishment, in a sign of betrayal. Yes, jealousy of two women fighting over the 'same grinding stone'. He bowed his head between his legs to avoid Stella's eyes and when he raised it up, Judy was being led away into the waiting prison van. Everybody stared at her till the vehicle vanished with her around a bend. And the people were left questioning themselves.

The End